DATE DUE

OCT 2 0 1995		
MAR 0 3 2000		
MAR 0 1 2018		
MAR 0 1 2018		

The Castle of Llyr

THE CASTLE OF

LLYR

by Lloyd Alexander

New York · Chicago · San Francisco

HOLT, RINEHART AND WINSTON

THE PRYDAIN CHRONICLES
BY LLOYD ALEXANDER ARE:

THE BOOK OF THREE

THE BLACK CAULDRON

THE CASTLE OF LLYR

TARAN WANDERER

THE HIGH KING

THE PRYDAIN PICTURE BOOKS
ILLUSTRATED BY EVALINE NESS ARE:

COLL AND HIS WHITE PIG

THE TRUTHFUL HARP

For the Friends of the
Companions, fondly.

Contents

The Castle of Llyr

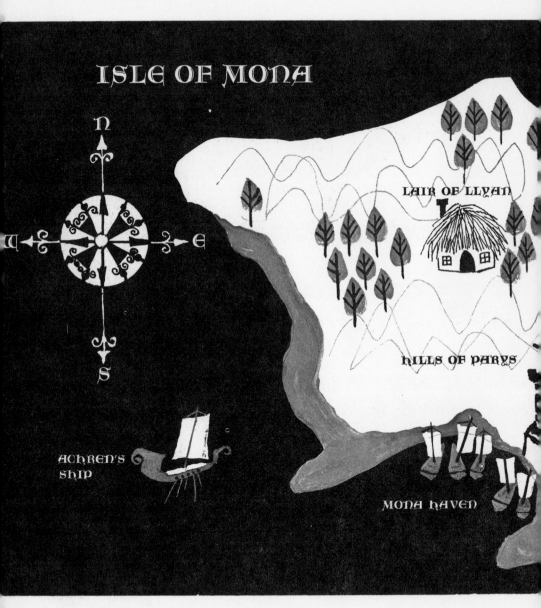

ISLE OF MONA

N

W   E

S

LAIR OF LLYAN

HILLS OF PARYS

ACHREN'S SHIP

MONA HAVEN

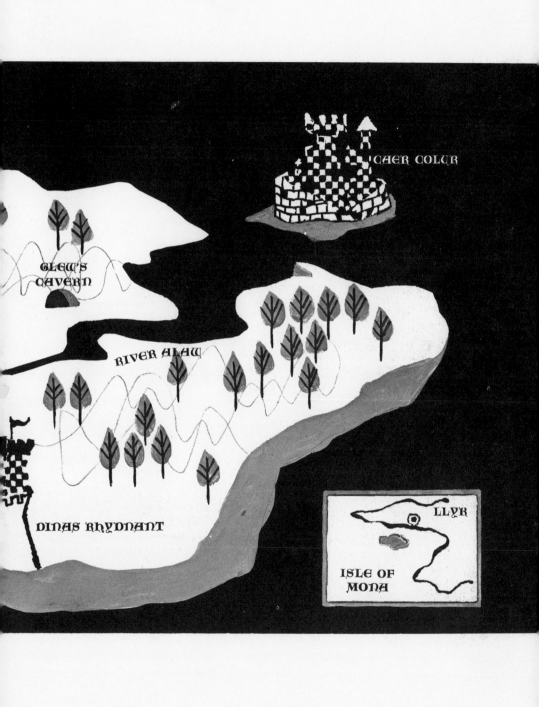

Author's Note

n this chronicle of Prydain, following *The Book of Three* and *The Black Cauldron,* what befalls the heroine is as important, and perilous, as the hero's own quest. Princess Eilonwy of the red-gold hair does much more than face the unavoidable (and, in her view, absolutely unnecessary) ordeal of becoming a young lady. As Dallben, the old enchanter, warns: "For each of us comes a time when we must be more than what we are." And this holds true for princesses as well as assistant pig-keepers.

The Castle of Llyr is, in a sense, more romantic than the preceding chronicles—Taran is noticeably aware of his feelings toward Eilonwy. And it is sometimes more comic—for example, the utter despair of the companions in trying to cope with the well-meaning but hapless Prince Rhun. The mood, perhaps, is bittersweet rather than grandly heroic. But the adventure should hold something beyond the fairy-tale elements of a magic golden bauble, a vengeful queen, a mysterious castle, and rivals for the hand of a princess. The nature of fantasy allows happenings which reveal most clearly our own frailties and our own strengths. The inhabitants of Prydain are fantasy figures; I hope they are also very human.

Prydain itself, however, is entirely imaginary. Mona, background for *The Castle of Llyr,* is the ancient Welsh name of the island of Anglesey. But this background is not drawn with a mapmaker's accuracy. My hope, instead, is to create the feeling, not the fact, of the land of Wales and its legends.

Some readers may indignantly question the fate of several villains in this tale, especially that of one of the most reprehensible scoundrels in Prydain. I should point out that while *The Castle of Llyr,* like the previous books, can stand as a chronicle in its own right, certain events in it have far-reaching consequences. Beyond that, I will hint no further but only recommend one of the more difficult virtues: patience.

—L.A.

CHAPTER I

Prince Rhun

Eilonwy of the red-gold hair, the Princess Eilonwy Daughter of Angharad Daughter of Regat of the Royal House of Llyr, was leaving Caer Dallben. Dallben himself had so ordered it; and though Taran's heart was suddenly and strangely heavy, he knew there was no gainsaying the old enchanter's words.

On the spring morning set for Eilonwy's departure, Taran saddled the horses and led them from the stable. The Princess, looking desperately cheerful, had wrapped her few belongings in a small bundle slung from her shoulder. At her neck hung a fine chain and crescent moon of silver; on her finger she wore a ring of ancient craftsmanship; and in the fold of her cloak she carried another of her most prized possessions: the golden sphere that shone at her command with a light brighter than a flaming torch.

Dallben, whose face was more careworn than usual and whose back was bowed as though under a heavy burden, embraced the girl at the cottage door. "You shall always have a place in Caer Dallben," he said, "and a larger one in my heart. But, alas, raising a young lady is a mystery beyond even an enchanter's skill. I have had," he added with a quick smile, "difficulties enough raising an Assistant Pig-Keeper.

"I wish you a fair voyage to the Isle of Mona," Dallben went on. "King Rhuddlum and Queen Teleria are kindly and gracious. They are eager to stand in your family's stead and serve as your protectors, and from Queen Teleria you shall learn how a princess should behave."

"What!" cried Eilonwy. "I don't care about being a princess! And since I'm already a young lady, how else could I behave? That's like asking a fish to learn how to swim!"

"Hem!" Dallben said wryly. "I have never seen a fish with skinned knees, torn robe, and unshod feet. They would ill become him, as they ill become you." He set a gnarled hand gently on Eilonwy's shoulder. "Child, child, do you not see? For each of us comes a time when we must be more than what we are." He turned now to Taran. "Watch over her carefully," he said. "I have certain misgivings about letting you and Gurgi go with her, but if it will ease your parting, so be it."

"The Princess Eilonwy shall go safely to Mona," Taran answered.

"And you," said Dallben, "return safely. My heart will not be at ease until you do." He embraced the girl again and went quickly into the cottage.

It had been decided that Coll would accompany them to Great Avren harbor and lead back the horses. The stout old warrior, already mounted, waited patiently. Shaggy-haired Gurgi, astride his pony, looked as mournful as an owl with a stomach ache. Kaw, the tame crow, perched in unwonted silence on Taran's saddle. Taran helped Eilonwy mount Lluagor, her favorite steed, then swung to the back of Melynlas, his silver-maned stallion.

Leaving Caer Dallben behind, the little band set out across the soft hills toward Avren. Side by side Taran and Coll rode ahead of the others to lead the way, Kaw meanwhile having made himself comfortable on Taran's shoulder.

"She never stopped talking for a moment," Taran said gloomily. "Now, at least, it will be quieter in Caer Dallben."

"That it will," said Coll.

"And less to worry about. She was always getting into one scrape or another."

"That, too," said Coll.

"It's for the best," Taran said. "Eilonwy is, after all, a Princess of Llyr. It's not as if she were only an Assistant Pig-Keeper."

"Very true," said Coll, looking off toward the pale hills.

They jogged along silently for a while.

"I shall miss her," Taran burst out at last, half angrily.

The old warrior grinned and rubbed his shining bald head. "Did you tell her that?"

"Not—not exactly," faltered Taran. "I suppose I should have. But every time I began talking about it I—I felt very odd. Besides, you never know what silly remark she'll come out with when you're trying to be serious."

"It may be," replied Coll, smiling, "we know least what we treasure most. But we will have more than enough to keep us busy when you come back, and you will learn, my boy, there is nothing like work to put the heart at rest."

Taran nodded sadly. "I suppose so," he said.

Past midday they turned their horses to the west, where the hills began a long slope downward into the Avren valley. At the last ridge Kaw hopped from Taran's shoulder and flapped aloft, croaking with excitement. Taran urged Melynlas over the rise. Below, the great river swung into view, wider here than he had ever seen it. Sunlight flecked the water in the sheltered curve of the harbor. A long, slender craft bobbed at the shore. Taran could make out figures aboard, hauling on ropes to raise a square, white sail.

Eilonwy and Gurgi had also ridden forward. Taran's heart leaped; and to all the companions the sight of the harbor and the waiting vessel was like a sea wind driving sorrow before it. Eilonwy began chattering gaily, and Gurgi waved his arms so wildly he nearly tumbled from the saddle.

"Yes, oh yes!" he cried. "Bold, valiant Gurgi is glad to follow kindly master and noble Princess with boatings and floatings!"

They cantered down the slope and dismounted at the water's edge. Seeing them, the sailors ran a plank out from the vessel to the shore. No sooner had they done so than a young man clambered onto the plank and hastened with eager strides toward the companions. But he had taken only a few paces along the swaying board when he lost his footing, stumbled, and with a loud splash pitched headlong into the shallows.

Taran and Coll ran to help him, but the young man had already picked himself up and was awkwardly sloshing his way ashore. He was of Taran's age, with a moon-round face, pale blue eyes, and straw-colored hair. He wore a sword and a small, richly ornamented dagger in a belt of silver links. His cloak and jacket, worked with threads of gold and silver, were now sopping wet; the stranger, however, appeared not the least dismayed either by his ducking or the sodden state of his garments. Instead, he grinned as cheerfully as if nothing whatever had befallen him.

"Hullo, hullo!" he called, waving a dripping hand. "Is that Princess Eilonwy I see? Of course! It must be!"

Without further ado, and without stopping even to wring out his cloak, he bowed so low that Taran feared the young man would lose his balance; then he straightened up and in a solemn voice declared: "On behalf of Rhuddlum Son of Rhudd and Teleria Daughter of Tannwen, King and Queen of the Isle of Mona, greetings to the Princess Eilonwy of the Royal House of Llyr, and to—well—to all the rest of you," he added, blinking rapidly as a thought suddenly occurred to him. "I should have asked your names before I started."

Taran, taken aback and not a little vexed by

this scatterbrained behavior, stepped forward and presented the companions. Before he could ask the stranger's name, the young man interrupted.

"Splendid! You must all introduce yourselves again later, one at a time. Otherwise, I might forget—oh, I see the shipmaster's waving at us. Something to do with tides, no doubt. He's always very concerned with them. This is the first time I've commanded a voyage," he went on proudly. "Amazing how easy it is. All you need to do is tell the sailors . . ."

"But who are you?" Taran asked, puzzled.

The young man blinked at him. "Did I forget to mention that? I'm Prince Rhun."

"*Prince* Rhun?" Taran repeated in a tone of disbelief.

"Quite so," answered Rhun, smiling pleasantly. "King Rhuddlum's my father; and, of course, Queen Teleria's my mother. Shall we go aboard? I should hate to upset the shipmaster, for he does worry about those tides."

Coll embraced Eilonwy. "When we see you again," he told her, "I doubt we shall recognize you. You shall be a fine Princess."

"I want to be recognized!" Eilonwy cried. "I want to be me!"

"Never fear," said Coll, winking. He turned to Taran. "And you, my boy, farewell. When you return, send Kaw ahead to tell me and I shall meet you at Avren harbor."

Prince Rhun, offering his arm to Eilonwy, led her across the plank. Gurgi and Taran followed them.

Having formed his own opinion of Rhun's agility, Taran kept a wary eye on the Prince until Eilonwy was safe aboard.

The ship was surprisingly roomy and well-fitted. The deck was long, with benches for oarsmen on either side. At the stern rose a high, square shed topped by a platform.

The sailors dipped their oars and worked the vessel to the middle of the river. Coll trotted along the bank and waved with all his might. The old warrior dropped from sight as the ship swung around a bend in the ever-widening river. Kaw had flapped to the masthead and, as the breeze whistled through his feathers, he beat his wings so pridefully that he looked more like a black rooster than a crow. The shore turned gray in the distance and the craft sped seaward.

If Rhun had perplexed and vaguely irritated him at their first meeting, Taran now began to wish he had never laid eyes on the Prince. Taran had meant to speak with Eilonwy apart, for there was much in his heart he longed to tell her. Yet each time he ventured to do so, Prince Rhun would pop up as if from nowhere, his round face beaming happily, calling out, "Hullo, hullo!"—a greeting Taran found more infuriating each time he heard it.

Once, the Prince of Mona eagerly dashed up to show the companions a large fish he had caught—to the delight of Eilonwy and Gurgi, but not Taran; for a moment later, Rhun's attention turned elsewhere and he hurried off, leaving Taran holding the wet, slippery fish in his arms. Another time, while leaning over the side to point out a school of dolphins, the Prince nearly dropped his sword into the sea. Luckily Taran caught it before the blade was lost forever.

After the ship reached open water Prince Rhun decided to take a hand at steering. But he no sooner grasped the tiller than it flew out of his fingers. While Rhun clutched at the wooden handle, the vessel lurched and slewed about so violently that Taran was flung against the bulwark. A water cask broke loose and went rolling down the deck, the sail flapped madly at the sudden change of course, and one bank of oars nearly snapped before the steersman regained the tiller from the undismayed Prince. The painful bump on Taran's head did nothing to raise his esteem of Prince Rhun's seamanship.

Although the Prince made no further attempt to steer the vessel, he climbed atop the platform where he called out orders to the crew.

"Lash up the sail!" Rhun shouted happily. "Steady the helm!"

No seaman himself, Taran nevertheless realized the sail was already tightly lashed and the craft was moving unwaveringly through the water; and he very shortly became aware that the sailors were quietly going about their task of keeping the ship on course without paying any heed whatever to the Prince.

Taran's head ached from the bump, his jacket was still unpleasantly damp and fishy, and when at last his chance came to speak with Eilonwy he was altogether out of sorts.

"Prince of Mona indeed!" he muttered. "He's no more than a—a princeling, a clumsy, muddle-headed baby. Commanding the voyage? If the sailors listened to him, we'd be aground in no time. I've never sailed a ship, but I've no doubt I could do it better than he. I've never seen anyone so feckless."

"Feckless?" answered Eilonwy. "He does often seem a little dense. But I'm sure he means well, and I've a feeling he has a good heart. In fact, I think he's rather nice."

"I suppose you do," Taran replied, all the more nettled by Eilonwy's words. "Because he gave you his arm to lean on? A gallant, princely gesture. Lucky he didn't pitch you over the side."

"It was polite, at least," Eilonwy remarked, "which is something Assistant Pig-Keepers sometimes aren't."

"An Assistant Pig-Keeper," Taran snapped. "Yes, that's to be my lot in life. I was born to be one, just as the Princeling of Mona was born to his rank. He's a king's son and I—I don't even know the names of my parents."

"Well," said Eilonwy, "you can't blame Rhun for being born. I mean, you could, but it wouldn't help matters. It's like kicking a rock with your bare foot."

Taran snorted. "I daresay that's his father's sword he's got on, and I daresay he's never drawn it except to frighten a rabbit. At least I've earned the right to wear mine. Yet he still calls himself a prince. Does his birth make him worthy of his rank? As worthy as Gwydion Son of Don?"

"Prince Gwydion's the greatest warrior in Prydain," Eilonwy replied. "You can't expect everyone to be like him. And it seems to me that if an Assistant Pig-Keeper does the best he can, and a prince does the best he can, there's no difference between them."

"No difference!" Taran cried angrily. "You spoke well enough of Rhun!"

"Taran of Caer Dallben," Eilonwy declared, "I really believe you're jealous. And sorry for yourself. And that's as ridiculous as—as painting your nose green!"

Taran said no more, but turned away and stared glumly at the water.

To make matters worse, the wind freshened, the sea heaved about the sides of the ship, and Taran could barely keep his footing. His head spun and he feared the vessel would capsize. Eilonwy, deathly pale, clung to the bulwark.

Gurgi wailed and howled pitifully. "Poor tender head is full of whirlings and twirlings! Gurgi does not like this ship any more. He wants to be at home!"

Prince Rhun appeared not the least distressed. He ate heartily and was in the best of spirits, while Taran huddled wretchedly in his cloak. The sea did not calm until dusk, and at nightfall Taran was grateful the vessel anchored in a calm cove. Eilonwy took out the golden sphere. In her hands it began to glow and its rays shimmered over the black water.

"I say, what's that?" cried Prince Rhun, who had clambered down from his platform.

"It's my bauble," said Eilonwy. "I always carry it with me. You never can tell when it will come in handy."

"Amazing!" exclaimed the Prince. "I've never seen anything like it in my life." He examined the golden ball carefully, but as he held it in his hand the light winked out. Rhun looked up in dismay. "I'm afraid I've broken it."

"No," Eilonwy assured him, "it's just that it doesn't work for everyone."

"Unbelievable!" said Rhun. "You must show it to my parents. I wish we had a few of those trinkets around the castle."

After a last, curious glance at the bauble, Rhun returned it to Eilonwy. Insisting that the Princess sleep in the comfort of the shed, Rhun bedded himself down amid a pile of netting. Gurgi curled up nearby, while Kaw, heedless of Taran's entreaties to leave his high perch, roosted on the mast. Rhun, falling asleep instantly, snored so piercingly that Taran, already vexed beyond endurance, stretched out on the deck as far as possible from the slumbering Prince. When Taran slept at last, he dreamed the companions had never left Caer Dallben.

CHAPTER II

Dinas Rhydnant

The days that followed put Taran in better spirits. The companions grew used to the motion of the ship; the air was clear, sharp, and salt-laden, and Taran could taste the briny spray on his lips. While Prince Rhun, from atop his platform, shouted commands which the crew, as usual, did not heed, the companions were glad to pass the time by lending a hand at the tasks aboard. The work, as Coll had foretold, eased Taran's heart. Yet there came moments when he suddenly recalled the purpose of the voyage and wished it would never end.

He had just finished coiling a length of rope when Kaw swooped down from the mast and circled around him, croaking wildly. An instant later the lookout cried they had sighted land. At Prince Rhun's urging, the companions hastened to climb to the platform. In the bright morning Taran saw the hills of Mona spring from the horizon. The vessel sped closer to the crescent-shaped harbor of Dinas Rhydnant, with its piers and jetties, its stone sea wall and clusters of ships. Steep cliffs rose almost from the water's

28

edge and on the highest of them stood a tall castle. From it, the banners of the House of Rhuddlum snapped in the breeze.

The vessel glided to the pier; the sailors cast the mooring lines and leaped ashore. The companions, with Prince Rhun marching in the lead, were escorted to the castle by ranks of warriors who made a hedge of honor with their spears.

Yet even this short journey did not end without mishap. The Prince of Mona, drawing his sword to return the salute of the Captain of Guards, did so with such a sweeping gesture that the point snagged in Taran's cloak.

"I say, I'm sorry about that," cried Rhun, curiously examining the long, gaping slash his blade had caused.

"And I, too, Prince of Mona," Taran muttered, vexed at Rhun and embarrassed at the impression his torn garment would make on the King and Queen. He said no more, but shut his lips and desperately hoped the damage would go unnoticed.

The procession passed through the castle gates and into a wide courtyard. Shouting a glad "Hullo, hullo!" Prince Rhun hurried to his waiting parents. King Rhuddlum had the same round and cheerful face as Prince Rhun. He greeted the companions cordially, repeating himself a number of times. If he was aware of Taran's torn cloak, he showed no sign, which only added to Taran's distress. When King Rhuddlum at last finished talking, Queen Teleria stepped forward.

The Queen was a stout, pleasant-looking

woman dressed in fluttering white garments; a golden circlet crowned her braided hair, which was the same straw color as Prince Rhun's. She showered Eilonwy with kisses, embraced the still embarrassed Taran, halted in amazement when she came to Gurgi, but embraced him nevertheless.

"Welcome, Daughter of Angharad," Queen Teleria began, returning to Eilonwy. "Your presence honors—don't fidget, child, and stand straight—our Royal House." The Queen stopped suddenly and took Eilonwy by the shoulders. "Good Llyr!" she cried. "Where did you get those frightful clothes? Yes, I can see it's high time Dallben let you out of that hole-and-corner in the middle of the woods."

"Hole-and-corner indeed!" Eilonwy cried. "I love Caer Dallben. And Dallben is a great enchanter."

"Exactly," said Queen Teleria. "He's so busy casting spells and all such that he's let you grow like a weed!" She turned to King Rhuddlum. "Wouldn't you say so, my dear?"

"Very much like a weed," agreed the King, eying Kaw with interest.

The crow hunched up his wings, opened his beak and loudly croaked "Rhuddlum!" to the King's immense delight.

Queen Teleria, meanwhile, had been examining Taran and Gurgi by turns. "Look at that disgracefully torn cloak! You must both have new raiment," she declared. "New jackets, new sandals, everything. Luckily we have a perfectly wonderful shoemaker at the castle now. He was just—don't pout that way, my child, you'll give yourself a blister—passing through. But we've kept him busy and he's still cobbling away. Our Chief Steward shall see to it. Magg?" she called. "Magg? Where is he?"

"At your command," answered the Chief Steward, who had been standing all the while by Queen Teleria's elbow. He wore one of the finest cloaks Taran had ever seen, its rich embroidery almost surpassing King Rhuddlum's garment. Magg carried a long staff of polished wood taller than himself, from his neck hung a chain of heavy silver links, and at his belt was a huge iron ring from which jingled keys of all sizes.

"All has been ordered," said Magg, bowing deeply. "Your decision has been foreseen. The shoemaker, the tailors and weavers stand ready."

"Excellent!" Queen Teleria cried. "Now, the Princess and I shall go first to the weaving rooms. And Magg shall show the rest of you to your chambers."

Magg bowed again, even more deeply, and beckoned with his staff. With Gurgi at his heels, Taran followed the Chief Steward through the courtyard, into a high stone building and down a vaulted corridor. At the end of it, Magg gestured toward an open portal and silently withdrew.

Taran stepped inside. The chamber was small, but neat and airy, bright with sunlight from a narrow casement. Fragrant rushes covered the floor and in one corner stood a low couch and pallet of straw. Taran had no sooner taken off his cloak when the portal suddenly burst open and a spiky, yellow head thrust in.

"Fflewddur Fflam!" Taran shouted with joyful surprise at the sight of this long-absent companion. "Well met!"

The bard seized Taran by the hand and began pumping it with all his might, at the same time clapping him resoundingly on the shoulder. Kaw flapped his wings while Gurgi leaped into the air, yelped at the top of his voice, and embraced Fflewddur in a shower of twigs, leaves, and shedding hair.

"Well, well, well!" said the bard. "And high time it is! I've been waiting for you. I thought you'd never get here."

"How did you come?" cried Taran, who had just begun to catch his breath. "How did you know we were to be at Dinas Rhydnant?"

"Why, I couldn't help knowing," the bard replied, beaming with delight. "There's been talk of nothing but the Princess Eilonwy. Where is she, by the way? I must find her and pay my respects at once. I was hoping Dallben would send you along with her. How is he? How is Coll? I see you've brought Kaw. Great Belin, I've seen none of you for so long I've lost track!"

"But Fflewddur," Taran interrupted, "what brings you to Mona, of all places?"

"Well, it's a short tale," said the bard. "I had decided, this time, really to make a go of being a king. And so I did, for the best part of a year. Then along came spring and the barding and wandering season, and everything indoors began looking unspeakably dreary, and everything outdoors began somehow pulling at me, and next thing I knew I was on my way. I'd never been to Mona, so that was the best reason in the world for going. I reached Dinas Rhydnant a week ago. The vessel had already left to meet you or you can be sure I'd have been on it."

"And you can be sure you'd have borne us better company than the Princeling of Mona," Taran said. "We were lucky that noble fool didn't somehow manage to blunder onto a reef and sink us in the tide. But what of Doli?" he went on. "I have longed to see him as much as I have longed to see you."

"Good old Doli." The bard chuckled, shaking his yellow head. "I tried to rouse him when I first set out. But he's hidden himself away with his kinsmen in the realm of the Fair Folk." Fflewddur sighed. "I fear our good dwarf has lost his taste for adventure. I managed to get word to him, thinking he might come along with me for the sport of it. He sent back a message. All it said was 'Humph!' "

"You should have come to meet us at the harbor," Taran said. "It would have cheered me to know you were here."

"Ah—yes, I was going to," replied Fflewddur, with some hesitation, "but I thought I'd wait and surprise you. I was busy, too, getting ready a song about the arrival of the Princess. Quite an impressive chant, if I do say so myself. We're all mentioned in it, with plenty of heroic deeds."

"And Gurgi, too?" cried Gurgi.

"Of course," said the bard. "I shall sing it for all of you this evening."

Gurgi shouted and clapped his hands. "Gurgi cannot wait to hear hummings and strummings!"

"You shall hear them, old friend," the bard assured him, "all in due course. But you can imagine I could hardly spare the time to join the welcoming procession . . ."

At this a harp string broke suddenly.

Fflewddur unslung his beloved instrument and looked at it ruefully. "There it goes again," he sighed. "These beastly strings will never leave off snapping whenever I—ah—add a little to the truth. And in this case, the truth of the matter is: I wasn't invited."

"But a bard of the harp is honored at every court in Prydain," Taran said. "How could they overlook—"

Fflewddur raised a hand. "True, true," he said. "I was certainly honored here, and handsomely, too. That was before they learned I wasn't a real bard. Afterward," he admitted, "I was moved into the stables."

"You should have told them you are a king," said Taran.

"No, no," said Fflewddur, shaking his head. "When I'm a bard, I'm a bard; and when I'm a king, that's something else again. I never mix the two.

"King Rhuddlum and Queen Teleria are decent sorts," Fflewddur continued. "The Chief Steward was the one who had me turned out."

"Are you sure there wasn't some mistake?" Taran asked. "From what I've seen of him, he seems to do his duties perfectly."

"All too well, if you ask me," said Fflewddur. "Somehow he found out about my qualifications, and next thing I knew—into the stables! The truth of it is I think he hates music. Surprising how many people I've run into who for some reason or other simply can't abide harp-playing."

Taran heard a loud rapping at the portal. It was Magg himself, come with the shoemaker, who stood humbly behind him.

"Not that he troubles me," Fflewddur whispered. "That is," he added, looking at the harp, "not beyond what I can honorably bear." He slung the instrument over his shoulder. "Yes, well, as I was saying, I must go and find Princess Eilonwy. We shall meet later. In the stables, if you don't mind. And I shall play my new song." Glaring at Magg, Fflewddur strode from the chamber.

The Chief Steward, taking no notice of the bard's angry glance, bowed to Taran. "As Queen Teleria commanded, you and your companion are to be given new apparel. The shoemaker will serve you as you wish."

Taran sat down on a wooden stool and, as Magg departed from the chamber, the shoemaker drew near. The man was bent with age and garbed most shabbily. A grimy cloth was wrapped around his head and a fringe of gray hair fell almost to his shoulders. At his broad belt hung curiously shaped knives, awls, and hanks of thongs. Kneeling before Taran, he opened a great sack and thrust in his hand to pull out strips of leather, which he placed about him on the floor. He squinted at his findings, holding up one after the other, then casting it aside.

"We must use the best, the best," he croaked, in a voice much like Kaw's. "Only that will do. To go well-shod is half the journey." He chuckled. "Is that not so, eh? Is that not so, Taran of Caer Dallben?"

Taran drew back with a start. The shoemaker's tone had suddenly rung differently. He stared down at the aged man who had picked up a piece of leather and was now shaping it deftly with a crooked little knife. The shoemaker, his face as tanned as his own materials, was watching him steadily.

Gurgi looked ready to yelp loudly. The man raised a finger to his lips.

Taran, in confusion, hurriedly knelt before the shoemaker. "Lord Gwydion . . ."

Gwydion's eyes flashed with pleasure, but his smile was grim. "Hear me well," he said quickly, in a hushed voice. "Should we be interrupted, I shall find a way to speak with you later. Tell no one who I am. What you must know, above all, is this: the life of the Princess Eilonwy is in danger. And so," he added, "is your own."

CHAPTER III

The Shoemaker

Taran paled. His head still whirled at seeing the Prince of Don in the guise of a shoemaker, and Gwydion's words left him all the more confused. "Our lives in danger?" he asked hurriedly. "Does Arawn of Annuvin seek us as far as Dinas Rhydnant?"

Gwydion motioned for Gurgi to stand guard at the portal and turned once more to Taran. "No," said Gwydion, with a quick shake of his head. "Though Arawn's wrath has grown to fury since the Black Cauldron was destroyed, the threat comes not from Annuvin."

Taran frowned. "Who then? There is none in Dinas Rhydnant who wishes us ill. You cannot mean that King Rhuddlum or Queen Teleria . . ."

"The House of Rhuddlum has always borne friendship to the Sons of Don and to our High King Math," replied Gwydion. "Look elsewhere, Taran of Caer Dallben."

"But who would harm Eilonwy?" Taran asked urgently. "It is known she is under Dallben's protection."

"There is one who would dare to stand against Dallben," Gwydion said. "One against whom my own powers may not suffice and whom I fear as much as Arawn himself." Gwydion's face was taut and his green eyes flickered with deep anger as he spoke one harsh word: "Achren."

Taran's heart chilled. "No," he whispered. "No. That evil enchantress is dead."

"So I, too, believed," Gwydion answered. "It is not true. Achren lives."

"She has not rebuilt Spiral Castle!" Taran cried, his thoughts flashing to the dungeon where Achren had held him prisoner.

"Spiral Castle still lies in ruins, as you left it," Gwydion said, "and grass already covers it. Oeth-Anoeth, where Achren would have given me to death, no longer stands. I have journeyed to those places and seen with my own eyes.

"You must know that I have long pondered her fate," Gwydion went on. "Of Achren there has not been the slightest sign, as though the earth had swallowed her. This troubled me and lay heavily on my heart, and I have never given up seeking traces of her.

"At last I found these traces," said Gwydion. "They were faint as words whispered in the wind, puzzling rumors that seemed at first no more than imaginings. A senseless riddle without an answer. Perhaps," Gwydion continued, "I should say an answer without a riddle. And it was only after long toil and hard journeying that I discovered part of that riddle. Alas, only a part."

Gwydion's voice lowered. As he spoke, his hands did not cease carving and shaping the unfinished sandal. "What I have learned is this. After Spiral Castle fell, Achren vanished. At first I believed she had sought refuge in the realm of Annuvin, for she had lived long as a consort of Arawn. Indeed, it was Achren who gave Arawn his power in the days when she herself ruled Prydain.

"But she did not go to Annuvin. Since she had let the sword Dyrnwyn slip from her hands, and failed to take my life, it may be that she feared Arawn's wrath. Perhaps she dared not face him, having been outwitted by a young girl and an Assistant Pig-Keeper. Of this, I am not certain. Nevertheless, she fled Prydain. Since then, no man knows what has befallen her. Yet even to know she is alive is cause enough for fear."

"Do you think she is on Mona?" Taran asked. "Does she seek vengeance on us? But Eilonwy was no more than a child when she escaped from Achren; she understood nothing of what she did."

"Wittingly or not, by taking Dyrnwyn from Spiral Castle, Eilonwy gave Achren her most grievous defeat," Gwydion said. "Achren does not forget or forgive." He knit his brows. "It is my fear that she seeks Eilonwy. Not only for revenge. I sense there is something other than that. It is hidden from me now, yet I must discover it without delay. More than Eilonwy's life may hang in the balance."

"If only Dallben had let her stay with us," Taran said in dismay. "He, too, must have known Achren was alive. Did he not realize Eilonwy would be in danger the moment she was beyond his protection?"

"Dallben's ways are deep," said Gwydion, "and not always given to me to fathom. He knows much, but he foresenses more than he chooses to tell." Gwydion, putting down his awl, drew out a leather thong and began stitching it through the sandal. "Dallben sent me word that the Princess Eilonwy would voyage to Mona, and counseled me to turn my attention here. He told me, too, of certain other matters. But it is better not to speak of them now."

"I cannot sit idle while Eilonwy may be in peril," Taran insisted. "Is there no way I can serve you?"

"You shall serve me best by keeping silent," Gwydion answered. "Stay watchful. Say nothing of me or of what we have spoken, not to the Princess Eilonwy, not even to Fflewddur." He smiled. "Our eager bard saw me in the stables and luckily did not know me. Meantime, I shall . . ."

Before the Prince of Don could finish, Gurgi began waving his arms in warning. Footsteps rang in the corridor and Gwydion bent quickly to the task of fitting the sandals.

"Hullo, hullo!" cried Prince Rhun, striding into the chamber. "Ah, shoemaker, there you are. Have you done with your work? I say, they are handsome, aren't they?" he said, glancing at the sandals. "Amazingly well-made. I should like a pair myself. Oh—my mother asks to see you in the Great Hall," he added, turning to Taran.

Gwydion's face had fallen suddenly into lines

and wrinkles; his shoulders were hunched and his voice shook with age. Without a further glance at Taran, Gwydion beckoned to Rhun. "Come with me, young Prince," he said. "you shall have sandals befitting your station."

As Kaw fluttered after him, Taran hurried from the chamber and down the corridor. Gurgi, round-eyed with fright, trotted beside him.

"Oh, fearsome danger!" Gurgi moaned. "Gurgi is sorry great enchanter sends us to place of peril. Gurgi wants to hide his poor tender head under kindly straw at Caer Dallben."

Taran warned him to silence. "Eilonwy is surely in more danger than we are," he whispered, hastening toward the Great Hall. "I don't like the thought of Achren turning up again any more than you do. But Gwydion is here to protect Eilonwy, and so are we."

"Yes, yes!" cried Gurgi. "Brave, loyal Gurgi will guard golden-haired Princess, too, oh yes; and she will be safe with him. But," he snuffled, "he still longs to be in Caer Dallben."

"Take heart, my friend," Taran said. He smiled and put a hand on Gurgi's trembling shoulder. "We companions shall see no ill befalls any of us. But remember—not a word that Gwydion is here. He has his own plans and we must do nothing to betray them."

"Gurgi will be silent!" Gurgi cried, clapping his hands to his mouth. "Oh, yes! But mind," he added, shaking a finger at Kaw, "that gossipy black bird does not tell with talkings and squawkings!"

"Silence!" Kaw croaked, bobbing his head. "Secrets!"

In the high-ceilinged Great Hall, with its flagstones that seemed to cover a space as large as the orchard at Caer Dallben, Taran caught sight of Eilonwy amid a group of court ladies. Some, of Eilonwy's age, were listening delightedly to the Princess; the rest, all of whom looked much like Queen Teleria, were frowning or whispering behind their hands. Magg, standing near the Queen's throne, watched impassively.

". . . and there we stood," Eilonwy was saying, her eyes flashing, "back to back, sword in hand! The Huntsmen of Annuvin burst from the forest! They were upon us in a moment!"

The young girls of the court gasped with excitement, while some of the older women gave horrified cluckings that reminded Taran of nothing so much as Coll's chicken run. Taran saw that Eilonwy wore a new cloak; her hair had been combed and dressed in a different fashion; among the ladies, she shone like a bird of golden plumage; and, with a curious twinge of heart, Taran realized that had it not been for her chattering he might not have known her.

"Good Llyr!" cried Queen Teleria, who had leaped from her throne as Eilonwy continued the tale of battle. "I'm beginning to think you haven't had a —my dear child, don't be so gleeful when you talk about hacking at people with swords—safe moment in your life." She blinked, shook her head, and fanned herself with a kerchief. "What a relief that Dallben has finally decided to be sensible and send you to us. If nothing else, you'll be out of harm's way."

Taran caught his breath, and it took all his strength to force himself not to shout Gwydion's warning aloud.

"Ah, there you are!" Queen Teleria called, spying Taran. "I had thought to speak to you about—that's right, young man, step up briskly, bow a little more deeply if you can, and, good Llyr, don't scowl so—the royal feast tonight. You shall be pleased to know that, in honor of all of you, we're planning to invite a perfectly wonderful bard, who claims to be a bard, that is, and who claims, by the way, to know you."

"The self-styled bard," said Magg, with ill-concealed distaste at the mention of Fflewddur, "has already been commanded to present himself at the feast."

"Therefore, in the matter of new garments," Teleria went on, "you had better go with Magg immediately and find some."

"That has been seen to, as well, Lady Teleria," murmured the Chief Steward, handing Taran a neatly folded cloak and jacket.

"Wonderful!" Teleria cried. "All that remains to be done is—well, I do believe everything *has* been done! I suggest, then, Taran of Caer Dallben, that you go and make yourself—don't frown so, you'll look old before your time—ready."

Taran hardly had finished bowing to Queen

Teleria when Eilonwy seized him and Gurgi by the arms and hastily drew them away. "You've seen Fflewddur, of course," she whispered. "Now it's getting to be more like old times. What a blessing to have him here! I've never met such silly women! Why, I don't think there's one of them that's ever drawn a sword! All they want to talk about is sewing and embroidery and weaving, and how to run a castle. The ones who have husbands are always complaining about them, and the ones who haven't are always complaining about the lack of them. They've never been out of Dinas Rhydnant in their lives! I told them a thing or two about some of our adventures; not the best ones—I'm saving those for later, when you can be there to tell your part in them.

"What we'll do," Eilonwy hurried on, her eyes sparkling, "after the feast, when no one's watching, we'll get hold of Fflewddur and go exploring for a few days. They'll never miss us; there's so many people coming and going around here. There's bound to be a few adventures on Mona, but we certainly won't find them in this stupid castle. Now, first thing, you must look out a sword for me—I wish I'd brought one from Caer Dallben. Not that I think we'll need swords, but it's better to have them just in case. Gurgi, of course, shall bring along his wallet of food—"

"Eilonwy," Taran interrupted, "this cannot be."

"How's that?" asked Eilonwy. "Oh, very well, you needn't bother with swords then. We'll just go adventuring as we are." She hesitated. "What's the matter with you? I must say, you have the strangest expressions on your face from time to time. Right now, you look as if a mountain were about to fall on your head. As I was saying . . ."

"Eilonwy," Taran said firmly, "you are not to leave Dinas Rhydnant."

Eilonwy, so surprised she stopped talking for a moment, stared at him open-mouthed. "What?" she cried. "What did you say? Not leave the castle? Taran of Caer Dallben, I think the salt air must have pickled your wits!"

"Listen to me," Taran said gravely, searching his mind for some means to warn the startled girl without revealing Gwydion's secret, "Dinas Rhydnant is—unfamiliar to us. We know nothing of Mona. There may be—dangers that we . . ."

"Dangers!" cried Eilonwy. "You can be sure of that! And the biggest is that I'll be bored to tears! Don't think for an instant I mean to wear out my days in this castle! You, of all people, tell me I'm not to go adventuring! What, really, is the matter with you? I'm ready to believe you dropped your courage over the side of Rhun's ship along with the anchor stone!"

"It is not a question of courage," Taran began. "It is the better part of wisdom to . . ."

"Now you're talking about wisdom!" Eilonwy cried. "Before, that was the last thing in the world you thought about!"

"This is different," Taran said. "Can you not understand?" he pleaded, though he saw clearly from Eilonwy's face that his words made no sense to her.

For an instant he was tempted to blurt out the truth. Instead, he took the girl by the shoulders. "You are not to set foot outside this place," he ordered angrily. "And if I think you have any idea of doing so, I shall ask King Rhuddlum to set a guard over you."

"What?" cried Eilonwy. "How dare you!" Tears suddenly filled her eyes. "Yes, I do understand! You're glad I've been sent to this wretched island and these clucking hens! You couldn't wait for a chance to be rid of me! You actually want me to stay here and be lost in this dreadful castle. That's worse than putting someone's head in a sack of feathers!" Sobbing, Eilonwy stamped her foot. "Taran of Caer Dallben, I'm not speaking to you any more!"

Shadows

The feast that evening was surely the merriest the
castle had ever seen. Kaw, perched on the back of
Taran's chair, bobbed up and down and looked as if
the banquet had been arranged entirely in his honor.
King Rhuddlum beamed with good spirits; the talk
and laughter of the guests rang through the Great
Hall. Behind the long table, crowded with Queen
Teleria's ladies of the court, Magg flitted back and
forth, snapping his fingers and whispering commands
to servitors bearing endless dishes of food and flagons
of drink. For Taran it was a waking nightmare; he sat
silent and uneasy, his repast untouched.

"You needn't look so gloomy," said Eilonwy.
"After all, you aren't the one who has to stay here. If
I'm trying to make the best of things, I must say
you're not exactly helpful. I want to remind you I'm
still not speaking to you after the way you behaved
today."

Without waiting to hear Taran's confused pro-
tests, Eilonwy tossed her head and began chattering
to Prince Rhun. Taran bit his lip. He felt as though he

47

were shouting a voiceless warning, while Eilonwy, all unwitting, raced gaily toward the brink of a cliff.

At the end of the feasting, Fflewddur tuned his harp, stepped to the middle of the Hall, and sang his new lay. Taran listened without pleasure, although he realized it was the best Fflewddur had yet composed. When the bard had done, and King Rhuddlum had begun to yawn, the guests rose from their seats at the table. Taran plucked Fflewddur's sleeve and drew him aside.

"I've been thinking about the stables," Taran said anxiously. "No matter what Magg says, it's not a fitting place for you to sleep. I'll speak to King Rhuddlum and I'm sure he'll order Magg to give you back your chamber in the castle." Taran hesitated. "I—I think somehow it would be better if we were all together. We are strangers here, and know nothing of the ways of this place."

"Great Belin, don't give yourself a moment's concern about that," replied the bard. "For my part, I prefer the stables. Indeed, that's one reason I go wandering: to get away from stuffy, dreary castles. Besides," he added behind his hand, "it would lead to trouble with Magg. And if he pushes me beyond endurance, there will be sword-play—a Fflam is hotheaded—which is hardly courteous behavior from a guest. No, no, we shall all be fine and meet again in the morning." So saying, Fflewddur shouldered his harp, waved good night, and made his way from the Hall.

"Something tells me we should keep an eye on

the castle," Taran said to Gurgi. He put a forefinger under Kaw's feet and set the bird on Gurgi's shoulder, where the crow immediately began running his beak through Gurgi's matted hair. "Stay close to Eilonwy's chamber," he went on. "I'll join you soon. Keep Kaw with you and send him to me if anything seems amiss."

Gurgi nodded. "Yes, yes," he whispered. "Loyal Gurgi will stand with watchful waitings. He will guard dreamful drowsings of noble Princess."

Unnoticed among the departing guests, Taran walked to the courtyard. Hoping to find Gwydion, he strode quickly toward the stables. Stars filled the clear night sky and a bright moon hung above the crags of Mona. In the stables, Taran discovered no trace of the Prince of Don, but came only upon Fflewddur curled up in the straw, his arm flung around his harp and already snoring peacefully.

Taran turned once more to the castle, which had by now fallen into darkness. He stood a moment, wondering where else he might seek.

"Hullo, hullo!" Prince Rhun burst from around a corner at such a rate he nearly sent Taran sprawling. "Still awake, are you? So am I! My mother says it's good for me to take a little stroll before sleeping. I suppose you're doing the same? Very good! We shall walk along together."

"That we shall not!" Taran retorted. Now, of all times, he had no wish to be hindered by the feckless Prince. "I—I seek the tailors," he added quickly. "Where are they lodged?"

"You're looking for tailors?" Rhun asked. "How odd! Whatever for?"

"My jacket," Taran hurriedly answered. "It— it fits me badly. I must ask them to fix it."

"In the middle of the night?" asked Rhun, his moon face puzzled. "Now, that really is surprising!" He pointed toward a shadowed side of the castle. "Their chambers are down there. But I shouldn't think they'd be in a humor to stitch well if you rouse them up out of a sleep. Tailors can be touchy, you know. I advise you to wait until morning."

"No, it must be done now," Taran said, impatient to be rid of Rhun.

The Prince shrugged, wished him a cheerful good night, and trotted off again. Taran made his way toward a cluster of sheds beyond the stable. His search there was also in vain. Discouraged, he had decided to rejoin Gurgi when he stopped suddenly. A figure was moving quickly across the courtyard, not toward the main portal but to the farthest angle of the heavy stone wall.

Could Eilonwy have slipped away from Gurgi? Taran was about to call out. Then, fearful of waking the castle, he hurried after the figure. An instant later it seemed to disappear completely. Taran pressed on. At the wall he stumbled upon a narrow opening, barely wide enough to squeeze through. Taran plunged through the curtain of ivy concealing it and found himself beyond the castle on a rocky slope overlooking the harbor.

50   The figure, Taran suddenly realized, was not

Eilonwy—too tall, the gait different. He caught his breath as the cloaked shape turned once for a furtive glance at the castle and the moonlight glittered for a moment over its features.

It was Magg.

Spider-like, the Chief Steward was rapidly picking his way down a path. In a surge of fear and suspicion, Taran clambered blindly over jagged stones, trying his best to be both swift and silent. Despite the clear night the way was difficult to follow, boulders loomed to catch him unawares and break his stride. He longed for the light of Eilonwy's bauble as he scrambled headlong after Magg toward the sleeping harbor.

Magg had come to level ground well ahead of Taran, and was scuttling along the sea wall until, at the far end, he reached a huge pile of rocks. With surprising agility the Chief Steward swung himself up, crawled over, and once more dropped out of sight. Casting caution aside, fearful he would lose track of Magg, Taran broke into a run. Along the wall moon-bright water lapped and whispered. A shadow moved for an instant among the stilted piers. In alarm Taran checked his pace, then hastened on. His eyes were playing tricks. Even the rocks themselves seemed to rise before him like crouching, threatening beasts.

Gritting his teeth, Taran climbed the dark barrier of rocks. Below, the water churned in glittering eddies and foamed among the stones. The surf rang in his ears as he hauled himself to the crest. There he clung, not daring to follow farther. Magg had stopped not many paces beyond, at the edge of a narrow spit of land. Taran saw him kneel and make a rapid motion. In another instant a light flared.

The Chief Steward had lit a torch and now raised it overhead, moving the flickering flame slowly back and forth. As Taran watched, fearful and puzzled, a tiny point of orange light glowed far seaward. This answering signal, Taran judged, could come only from a ship, though he could make out nothing of the vessel's shape or distance. Magg waved the torch again, in a different pattern. The light from the ship repeated it, then winked out. Magg thrust his torch into the black water where it sputtered and died; he turned and strode quickly toward the tumble of rocks where Taran lay. Taran, left blinking in the sudden darkness, sought to clamber down before Magg should come upon him, but could find no foothold. In panic he groped for a jutting stone below him, slipped, caught vainly for another one. He could hear Magg scrabbling up the far side and let himself fall among the rocks. Wincing at the sharp pain, he tried to hide in the shadows. Magg's head had just appeared at the crest when Taran was seized firmly from behind.

Taran snatched at his sword. A hand was clapped over his mouth, stifling his shout, and he was dragged rapidly toward the foaming wavelets, to be flung silently down amid the stones.

"Make no sound!" Gwydion's voice whispered the command.

Taran went limp with relief. Overhead, Magg

lowered himself from the mass of stones and passed no more than a dozen paces from the two crouching figures. Gwydion, clinging to the rocks above the surf, motioned for Taran to stay hidden. The Chief Steward, without a backward glance, hastened once more along the sea wall, heading for the castle.

"Seize him!" Taran urged. "A ship rides at anchor. I saw him signal it. We must make him tell us what he is about."

Gwydion shook his head. His green eyes followed the retreating Magg and his lips drew tightly against his teeth in the lean smile of a stalking wolf. He still wore the rags of the shoemaker; but Dyrnwyn, the black sword, now hung at his belt. "Let him go," he murmured. "The game is not played out."

"But the signal," Taran began.

Gwydion nodded. "I, too, saw it. I have been keeping watch over the castle since I left you. Though a moment ago," he added, with some severity, "I feared an Assistant Pig-Keeper would stumble into a snare set to catch a traitor. Would you serve me? Then return at once to the castle. Stay close by the Princess."

"Dare we let Magg go unhindered?" Taran asked.

"He must go unhindered for a time, at least," replied Gwydion. "The shoemaker will soon put down his awl and take up the sword. Until then, keep silent. I would not spoil Magg's scheme before I learn more of it.

"The fisherfolk of Mona have already told a

curious and harmless shoemaker part of what he must know," Gwydion continued. "Enough to be certain of one thing: Achren is aboard that vessel.

"Yes," Gwydion went on as Taran drew a sharp breath, "this much I suspected. Achren herself would not dare strike directly against Eilonwy. The castle is strong and well-guarded, only treachery could open its gates. Achren needed a hand to do her bidding. Now I know whose it is."

Gwydion frowned deeply as he spoke on. "But why?" he murmured almost to himself. "Too much still remains hidden. If it is as I fear . . ." He shook his head quickly. "It does not please me to use Eilonwy as unwitting bait for a trap, but I cannot do otherwise."

"Magg can be watched," Taran said, "but what of Achren?"

"I must find some means to learn her plan as well as Magg's," replied Gwydion. "Go quickly now," he ordered. "Soon all may grow clear. So I hope, for I would not see the Princess Eilonwy long in peril."

Taran hastened to obey Gwydion's command. Leaving the Prince of Don at the harbor, he made his way with all speed up the winding path to the castle, found the opening in the wall, and pressed through it into the dark courtyard. Eilonwy, he knew, would not be safe so long as Magg had the freedom of the castle. But Magg, at least, could be watched. The terror that chilled Taran's heart came from the ship waiting in the night. Memory of Achren, beautiful and merciless, again returned to him. From a day long past he recalled her livid face, her voice that had spoken so softly of torment and death. It was her shadow that loomed behind the treacherous Chief Steward.

He hurried silently across the courtyard. A dim light shone from one of the chambers. Stealthily, Taran moved toward it, raised himself on tiptoe, and peered through the casement. In the glow of an oil lamp he saw the Chief Steward. Magg clutched a long dagger which he brandished in the air, all the while making fierce grimaces. After a time he hid the weapon in his garments, then picked up a small looking glass into which he smiled, pursed his lips, and eyed himself with glances of deep satisfaction. Taran watched with rage and horror, hardly able to keep from bursting in upon him. With a final smirk, the Chief Steward put out the lamp. Taran clenched his fists, turned away, and entered the castle.

At Eilonwy's chamber he found Gurgi crouched on the flagstones. Rumpled and half-asleep, Gurgi blinked and sprang to his feet. Kaw, as tousled as Gurgi himself, popped his head from under his wing.

"All is quiet," Gurgi whispered. "Yes, yes, watchful Gurgi has not moved from portal! Valiant, sleepy Gurgi keeps noble Princess from harmful hurtings. His poor tender head is heavy, but it does not nod, oh no!"

"You have done well," Taran said. "Sleep, my friend. Go and rest that poor tender head of yours and I shall stay here until daylight."

While Gurgi, yawning and rubbing his eyes,

crept down the corridor, Taran took his place before the chamber. He sank to the flagstones and, with hand on sword, rested his head on his knees and fought against his own weariness. Once or twice, despite his efforts, he drowsed, then started up suddenly. The vaulted corridor slowly lightened in the rising dawn. With relief Taran saw the first rays of morning and at last allowed himself to close his eyes.

"Taran of Caer Dallben!"

He stumbled to his feet and clutched his blade. Eilonwy, looking fresh and well-rested, stood in the doorway.

"Taran of Caer Dallben!" she declared. "I nearly tripped over you! Whatever in the world are you doing?"

Befuddled, Taran could only stammer that he found the hallway more comfortable than his chamber.

Eilonwy shook her head. "That," she remarked, "is the silliest thing I've heard this morning. I may hear something sillier, because it's early yet, but I doubt it. I'm beginning to think the ways of Assistant Pig-Keepers are quite beyond me." She shrugged. "In any case, I'm going to breakfast. After you wash your face and untangle your hair, you might have some too. It would do you good. You look as jumpy as a frog with fleas!"

Without waiting for Taran to shake the sleep from his head, and before he could stop her, Eilonwy disappeared down the corridor. Taran hurried after her. Even in the bright morning he felt shadows cling to him like black spider webs. By now, he hoped,

Gwydion had discovered Achren's plan. But Magg still went free. Taran, recalling the Chief Steward's hidden dagger, had no intention of letting Eilonwy out of his sight for an instant.

"Hullo, hullo!" His round face glowing as if he had just scrubbed it, Prince Rhun popped out of his chamber just as Taran passed by. "Going to breakfast?" cried the Prince, clapping Taran on the shoulder. "Good! So am I."

"Then we shall meet in the Great Hall," Taran hastily replied, striving to shake himself loose from Rhun's friendly grasp.

"Amazing how one's appetite grows during the night," Prince Rhun went on. "Oh, by the way, did you ever manage to rouse the tailors?"

"Tailors?" Taran answered impatiently. "What tailors? Oh—yes, yes, they have done what I asked," he quickly added, peering down the corridor.

"Splendid!" cried Rhun. "I wish I had the same good fortune. Do you know, that shoemaker never did finish my sandals? He'd only just begun, then off he went, and that was the end of them."

"It may be he had a more important task to do," Taran replied. "As do I—"

"What could be more important to a shoemaker than making shoes?" asked Rhun. "However . . ." He snapped his fingers. "Ah! I knew there was something. I've forgotten my cloak. Hold on, I shall only be a moment."

"Prince Rhun," Taran cried, "I must join the Princess Eilonwy."

"We shall be there directly," called Rhun from

the chamber. "Oh, drat! There goes my sandal lace broken! I do wish that shoemaker had finished his work!"

Leaving the Prince of Mona still rummaging in the chamber, Taran sped anxiously to the Great Hall. King Rhuddlum and Queen Teleria were already at table, the Queen surrounded, as always, by her ladies. Taran looked quickly about him. Magg, usually in attendance, was not there.

Nor was there any sign of Eilonwy.

CHAPTER V

The Oath

"Where is Eilonwy?" Taran cried, as King Rhuddlum and Queen Teleria stared at him in astonishment. "Where is Magg? He's made off with her! Sire, I beg you. Turn out your guard. Help me find them. Eilonwy is in danger of her life!"

"What, what?" Queen Teleria clucked. "Magg? The Princess? You're overwrought, young man. Perhaps the sea air—don't shake so and wave your arms about—has gone to your head. Because someone isn't here for breakfast doesn't mean they're in danger. Does it, my dear?" she asked, turning to the King.

"I should hardly think so, my dear," answered Rhuddlum. "This is a heavy charge to bring against a loyal retainer," he added, looking gravely at Taran. "Why do you accuse him?"

For a moment, Taran stood perplexed and torn. Gwydion had bound him to secrecy. But now that Magg had struck, must the secret still be kept? Taking his decision, he let the words tumble from his lips, hurriedly and often confusedly telling all that had happened since the companions had reached Dinas Rhydnant.

Queen Teleria shook her head. "This shoe-maker disguised as Prince Gwydion—or was it the other way around—and ships and torch signals to enchantresses make the wildest tale I've heard, young man."

"Wild indeed," said King Rhuddlum. "But we shall learn the truth easily enough. Fetch the shoe-maker and we shall soon see if he is the Prince of Don."

"Prince Gwydion seeks Achren," Taran cried. "I have given you the truth. If it is not so, you shall take my life for it. Will you prove my words? Fetch your Chief Steward."

King Rhuddlum frowned. "It is odd that Magg should not be here," he admitted. "Very well, Taran of Caer Dallben. He shall be found and you shall re-peat your tale in his presence." He clapped his hands and ordered a servitor to summon the Chief Steward.

Frantic with anxiety, knowing that time was fleeting and delay could cost Eilonwy's life, Taran was nearly beside himself when the servitor at last re-turned with tidings that Magg appeared to be no-where in the castle, nor could Eilonwy be found. As King Rhuddlum hesitated, still puzzled by Taran's words, Gurgi, Kaw, and Fflewddur entered the Great Hall. Taran raced to them.

"Magg! That villainous spider!" the bard ex-claimed as soon as Taran told him what had hap-pened. "Great Belin, she's ridden off with him! I saw them galloping through the gate. I called to her, but she didn't hear me. She seemed cheerful enough. I'd no idea anything was amiss. But they're gone, long gone by now!"

Queen Teleria turned deathly pale. The ladies of the court gasped fearfully. King Rhuddlum sprang to his feet. "You have spoken the truth, Taran of Caer Dallben."

Shouting for the guard, the King strode from the Great Hall. The companions hastened after him. At King Rhuddlum's hurried orders, the stables were flung open. Within moments the courtyard filled with warriors and neighing horses. Prince Rhun, meantime, had strolled into the courtyard where he peered at the gathering host.

"Hullo, hullo!" he called to Taran. "Is this a hunting party? Splendid thought. I should enjoy a brisk morning ride."

"A hunt for your traitor steward," Taran retorted, thrusting Rhun aside and making his way to King Rhuddlum. "Sire, where is your war leader? Give us leave to put ourselves at his service."

"My war leader, sorry to say, is none other than Magg himself," the King answered. "As we've never had a war on Mona, we never needed a war leader, and it seemed quite in order to give Magg the honorary title. I shall form up the searching party myself. As for you—yes—by all means help with any tasks that need doing."

While King Rhuddlum saw to the ordering of the warriors, Taran and the companions labored with all speed, tightening saddle girths and handing out weapons from the armory. Prince Rhun, Taran saw, had clambered astride a swaybacked, piebald mare that persisted in turning in circles despite the efforts of the Prince to control her. Fflewddur and Gurgi had led out three horses. A glance at the animals filled Taran with despair, for they seemed unspirited, of no great mettle, and he wished for the swift-footed Melynlas now grazing peacefully at Caer Dallben.

King Rhuddlum, taking Taran by the arm, drew him hurriedly into an empty stable. "You and I must speak together," the King said quickly. "The warriors are ready and divided into two parties. One I shall lead over the lands south of the River Alaw. You and your companions are to ride with my son, who shall command the search in the Hills of Parys north of the Alaw. It is of him I would speak."

"Prince Rhun in command?" Taran burst out.

"What then, Taran of Caer Dallben," King Rhuddlum asked sharply. "Do you question Prince Rhun's skill?"

"Skill!" Taran cried. "He has none! Eilonwy's life hangs in the balance; our task must be done without delay. Give command to a feckless fool? He can barely knot a sandal lace, let alone ride a horse or wield a sword. The voyage to Mona showed me more than enough. Choose one of your liege men, a warrior, a forester, anyone save Rhun . . ." He stopped short. "Dallben has my oath to protect Eilonwy, and I say what is in my heart. Were I to say less, I would fail my duty. If I am to suffer for my words, then so be it."

"Once again you speak the truth," King Rhuddlum answered. "It is not you who suffers for it, but I." He put a hand on Taran's shoulder. "Think you I do not know my own son? You are right in your judgment. But I know, too, that Rhun must grow to be both a man and a king. You carry the burden of an oath to Dallben. I pray you take the burden of another one.

"Word of your deeds has reached Mona," King Rhuddlum went on, "And I have seen for myself that you are a brave lad, and honorable. I confide this knowledge to you: my Master of Horse is a skillful tracker; he rides with your party and in truth shall direct the search. Prince Rhun commands in name only, for the warriors expect leadership from the Royal House. I would entrust my son to you, and beg you to let no harm befall him. Nor," added the King, smiling sadly, "to let him make too great a fool of himself. Much he has to learn, and much, perhaps, he may learn from you. One day he must be King of Mona, and it is my hope he will rule honorably and wisely with Eilonwy his Queen."

"Eilonwy?" Taran cried, "with Rhun her husband?"

"Yes," answered King Rhuddlum. "When the Princess comes of age, it is our desire they shall wed."

"Princess Eilonwy," Taran murmured, confused. "Does she know of this?"

"Not yet. Nor does my son," said King Rhuddlum. "Eilonwy must have time to grow used to Mona and our ways here. But I am sure it will be happily arranged. After all, she is a Princess and Rhun is of royal blood."

Taran bowed his head. The grief in his heart kept him from speaking.

"What say you, Taran of Caer Dallben?" King Rhuddlum asked. "Will you give me your word?"

From the courtyard Taran could hear the clamor of warriors and the voice of Fflewddur calling his name. Yet these sounds reached his ears as though from a great distance. He remained silent, his eyes downcast.

"In this, I do not speak as liege lord to liege man," King Rhuddlum added. "I speak as a father who loves his son." He paused, watching Taran closely.

At last Taran met the King's eyes. "I will swear this oath," he said slowly. "Your son will come to no harm if it lies in my power to keep him from it." Taran put a hand to his sword. "I pledge my life to do so."

"Go with my thanks, Taran of Caer Dallben," King Rhuddlum said. "And help us bring the Princess Eilonwy safely home."

The bard and Gurgi were already mounted when Taran hurried from the stable. Heavy-hearted, he swung into the saddle. Kaw flew to join him. Prince Rhun, who had finally managed to keep his steed from turning in circles, was shouting commands, unheeded

as usual.

As the searching parties galloped out the gates, Taran lifted Kaw from his shoulder. "Can you find her? Seek her carefully, my friend," he murmured, while the crow cocked his head and looked at Taran with shrewd eyes. Taran flung his arm upward. Kaw launched himself into the air and sped aloft. Wings beating, the crow circled overhead, drove higher against the sky, then disappeared from sight.

"Yes, yes!" shouted Gurgi, waving his arms. "Go with flyings and spyings! Lead us to evil, wicked steward!"

"The sooner the better!" cried Fflewddur. "I can't wait to get my hands on that sneering spider. He shall know the fury of a Fflam!"

Glancing behind him, Taran saw King Rhuddlum's band stream from the castle and turn southward. Ahead, the Master of Horse led his party of warriors toward the higher ground above Dinas Rhydnant and signaled for the outriders to search for tracks. Taran's face was set and grim as he rode silently next to Fflewddur.

"Have no fear," the bard assured him, "we shall bring Eilonwy back with us safe and sound before nightfall, and all of us shall make merry over this adventure. I promise you a new song in celebration!"

"You would do well to make it a chant of betrothal," Taran said bitterly, "and sing of the wedding of the Prince of Mona."

"Rhun?" cried the startled Fflewddur. "To be wed? I had no idea! That's one disadvantage of being lodged in the stables instead of the castle, you miss the news and gossip. Prince Rhun, indeed! Who is to be his bride?"

Painfully, Taran told the bard of King Rhuddlum's plans and of his own oath to keep Rhun from harm.

"Oho," said Fflewddur, when Taran had finished, "so that's the way the wind blows! Strange," he added, with a quick glance at Taran, "I had always hoped that if Eilonwy were betrothed to anyone it would be—yes, well, what I mean to say is that despite all the squabbling and bickering between the two of you, I had rather expected . . ."

"Do not mock me," Taran burst out, reddening. "Eilonwy is a Princess of the House of Llyr. You know my station as well as I. Such a hope has never been in my mind. It is only fitting for Eilonwy to be betrothed to one of her own rank." Angrily he drew away from the bard and galloped ahead.

"So you say, so you say," murmured Fflewddur, hurrying after him. "Look closer into your heart. You may find your opinion to be somewhat different."

Taran, unhearing, pressed his steed to join the line of warriors.

Turning northward along the lower slopes of the Hills of Parys, the searching party broke into smaller bands, each quartering its own ground. The warriors, widely separated, moved in long, wavering lines, often out of each other's sight, painstakingly scouting every possible hiding place. Yet, as the morning wore away and noontide passed, they found no trace of the Chief Steward or Eilonwy.

Among the green and gentle slopes ran broken, pebbly trails, where the fleeing Magg might have passed and where clues would be invisible to the eyes of even the most able tracker. Taran's heart sank; in his mind chafed the fear that he was following a false hope and that Eilonwy had been taken in an altogether different direction. From time to time he anxiously scanned the sky for a glimpse of Kaw returning with news of the Princess.

Gwydion, Taran knew, was the only one who might discover Achren's plan. Magg was the key, but the Chief Steward had acted so swiftly that perhaps even now he was beyond the reach of the searching party. Taran redoubled his efforts to find a broken twig, a loose stone—anything that might bring them closer to Eilonwy before nightfall put an end to the day's searching.

Gurgi, riding close at hand, called out to him. "Look, look! Noble prince goes far alone, too far into the woods! He will lose himself. Then cheerful hullos will turn to sad moanings and groanings!"

Taran, who had dismounted to study what seemed a possible trail, raised his eyes in time to see Prince Rhun galloping over the shoulder of a hill. He shouted at him, but Rhun was too distant to hear, or, more likely, Taran thought, was simply paying no heed. He leaped astride his horse and sought to overtake the Prince. Until now he had managed to keep Prince Rhun always in view, but by the time Taran reached the hill, Rhun had vanished into the shadows of an alder grove. Below, on the rapidly darkening meadow, Fflewddur had cantered into sight and was calling him. Taran shouted Rhun's name once again, then beckoned for the bard and Gurgi to join him.

"That sickening spider has escaped us today," Fflewddur cried angrily, while his nag labored to the crest. "But we shall fetch him out tomorrow and Eilonwy will be safe and sound. If I know the Princess, Magg has already begun to regret stealing her away. She's worth a dozen warriors even if she's tied hand and foot!" Despite the bard's brave words, his face looked deeply worried. "Come," said Fflewddur, "the Master of Horse is calling in the warriors. We're to make camp with them for the night."

Even as the bard spoke, Taran heard the faint notes of a signal horn. He frowned. "I dare not leave Prince Rhun to wander alone in the forest."

"In that case," replied Fflewddur, glancing toward the setting sun, "we had best get hold of him without delay. A Fflam is keen-eyed! But I'd rather not go stumbling about the countryside after dark, if it can possibly be avoided."

"Hasten, yes, yes, with hurryings and scurryings!" cried Gurgi. "Fearsome shadows fall, and bold but cautious Gurgi does not know what hurtful things hide in them!"

The companions rode quickly into the grove where, Taran felt certain, they would find the Prince.

However, once beyond the ring of alders, and seeing nothing of him, Taran's alarm grew. Vainly he called the Prince's name. Only the echo returned.

"He cannot have ridden far," he told the bard. "Even Rhun would have wits enough to halt at nightfall."

Darkness covered the grove. The horses, more used to their quiet stalls in Dinas Rhydnant than to the forests of Mona, trod fearfully, rearing and shying at every wind-stirred bush. The companions were obliged to dismount and make their way on foot, leading the reluctant steeds. By this time Taran was deeply troubled. What had begun as a simple matter had turned grave.

"He might have fallen from his horse," Taran said. "Even now he might be lying hurt or unconscious."

"Then I suggest we find our way back to the rest of the band," said Fflewddur, "and ask them to help us. In this gloom the more eyes the better."

"We would lose too much time," Taran answered, pressing on through the underbrush. Gurgi followed, whimpering softly to himself. The rising ground told Taran they were moving above the foothills. No sound came but the hiss of saplings that whipped back as he passed and the click of the horses' hooves over pale stones. Taran stopped short, his heart in his mouth. From a corner of his eye he glimpsed a fleeting movement. It lasted but an instant, a shadow within a shadow. Fighting down his fear, he groped ahead. The horses had turned more skittish than before, and Taran's mount laid back his ears and voiced a frightened whinny.

Gurgi, too, had sensed the dark presence. The terrified creature's hair rose along his neck and he began to howl pitifully. "Wicked, evil things come to follow harmless Gurgi! Oh, kind master, save Gurgi's poor tender head from hurtful dangers!"

Taran drew his sword and the companions, with many backward glances into the darkness, hurried on. This time the horses did not lag, but plunged desperately ahead, nearly dragging the bard with them.

"Great Belin!" protested Fflewddur, who had crashed into a tree and struggled to free his jangling harp from a bush, "hold up, there! Next thing you know, we'll be looking for our own steeds as well as for Prince Rhun!"

With difficulty Taran managed to calm the animals who now refused to budge. Despite all his coaxing, pleading, and tugging, the horses stood stiff-legged and round-eyed, their flanks trembling. Taran, himself exhausted, sank to the ground.

"Our search is blind and useless," he said. "You were right," he went on, turning to Fflewddur. "We should have gone back. The time I had hoped to save is wasted twice over, and Eilonwy's danger is greater with every moment we delay. Now Prince Rhun is lost—and so is Kaw, for all we know."

"I'm afraid you're right," sighed Fflewddur. "And unless you or Gurgi knows where we are, I rather suspect we're lost, too."

CHAPTER VI

The Potions of Glew

At these words Gurgi set up a wail and rocked back and forth, clutching his head. Taran swallowed his own despair as best he could and tried to reassure the frightened creature.

"We can do nothing now but wait for dawn," Taran said. "The Master of Horse cannot be too far away. Find him as soon as you can. Above all, do not delay the search for Eilonwy. I shall seek Prince Rhun," he added bitterly. "I have given my oath to keep him from harm and I cannot do otherwise. But when I find him, I'll rejoin you somehow."

He was silent then, his head bowed. Fflewddur was watching him. "Do not wear out your heart with grief," the bard said quietly. "Magg can't escape us for long. I don't believe he means to harm Eilonwy but only bring her to Achren. And we shall catch him long before he can do that. Rest now. Gurgi and I will share the watch."

Too weary to protest, Taran stretched out on the ground and covered himself with his cloak. No sooner did his eyes close than fears of Achren came to torment him. In rage and vengeance the haughty

Queen would slay any of the companions who fell into her hands. And Eilonwy? He dared not let himself imagine her in Achren's grasp. When at last he dropped into fitful slumber it was as though he slept beneath a millstone.

The sun had barely risen when he opened his eyes with a start. Fflewddur was shaking him. The bard's yellow hair stood out raggedly in all directions, his face was pale with fatigue, but he grinned broadly.

"Good news!" he cried. "Gurgi and I have done some seekings and peekings of our own. We're not as badly lost as you might think. The truth of it is we've been thrashing around in a circle. Look for yourself."

Taran sprang to his feet and followed the bard to a low ridge. "You're right. There's the alder grove. It must be! And there—I remember the fallen tree where I lost sight of Rhun. Come," he added, "we shall ride that far together. Then you must go ahead and catch up with the rest of the band."

Hastily the companions mounted and urged their steeds toward the grove. Before they reached it, Taran's horse drew up sharply, then bore suddenly to the left. A loud whinny rose from the cover of trees along the shoulder of a hill. In astonishment, Taran slackened the reins and let the horse canter freely toward the sound. In another few moments he glimpsed a pale shape beyond the foliage. As the steed carried him closer, he recognized Rhun's piebald mare.

"See there!" he called to Fflewddur. "Rhun

can't be far. We must have gone by him during the night."

Reining up, he leaped from the saddle. His heart sank. The horse stood riderless. At the sight of the other steeds, she raised her head, shook her mane, and whickered anxiously.

Fearing the worst, Taran hurried past the mare while Fflewddur and Gurgi dismounted and raced after him. He stopped short. Before him, in a clearing, stood something that looked at first like a huge straw beehive. Fflewddur by then had come up beside him. Taran raised a hand in warning and moved cautiously toward the strange hut.

The conical thatched roof, he now saw, had fallen away in many places. Rough stones, piled one on top of the other, formed a low side wall, a corner of which had collapsed into a heap of rubble. There were no windows, and the single, heavy door hung askew from sagging leather hinges. He stepped closer. The holes in the thatch stared at him like empty eyes.

Fflewddur glanced about him. "I'm not too fond of going up and rapping on the door," he whispered, "and asking whoever's inside whether they've happened to see the Prince of Mona. Somehow, it seems the kind of place even Rhun would rather avoid. But I suppose there's no other way to find out."

Just then the door was flung open from the inside. Gurgi, with a yell, sought safety by scrambling
up a tree. Taran's hand went to his sword.

"Hullo, hullo!" Prince Rhun, beaming, stood in the doorway. Aside from looking a little sleepy, he appeared quite himself and altogether unharmed. "I hope you've got some breakfast with you," he added, rubbing his hands eagerly. "I'm nearly starved to death. Have you ever noticed how the fresh air sharpens one's appetite? Most surprising!

"Come in, come in," Rhun went on, while Taran stared speechless at him. "You'd be amazed how comfortable it is. Surprisingly snug and cozy. Where did the rest of you pass the night? I hope you slept as well as I did. You can't imagine . . ."

Taran could control himself no longer. "What have you done?" he burst out. "Why did you leave the searching party? Count yourself lucky that getting lost was the worst that happened to you!"

Prince Rhun blinked and looked puzzled. "Leave the searching party?" he asked. "Why, I didn't actually leave it. Not on purpose, you understand. It happened when I fell off my horse and had to go chasing after her all over nowhere, until I found her near this hut. By then it was getting dark, so I went to sleep. That's only common sense, wouldn't you say? I mean, why sleep outdoors when you can put a roof over your head?

"As far as being lost goes," Rhun went on, "it seems to me *you're* the ones who got lost. Wherever I go, that's where the search is, if you see what I mean. After all, the one who's in command . . ."

"Yes, you command," Taran flung back angrily, "as you were born to, as a king's son." He stopped abruptly. Another instant and he would have cried aloud his promise to King Rhuddlum, and his oath to protect this witless Prince. Taran clenched his teeth. "Prince Rhun," he said coldly, "you need not remind us we are under your orders. But for your own safety, I urge you to stay close to us."

"And I advise you to stay away from strange huts," put in Fflewddur. "Last time I was in one, I almost got changed into a toad." The bard shook his head. "Shun them—huts, that is," he added. "You never know what disagreeable thing you'll run into— and by the time you find out, it's too late."

"Changed into a toad?" cried Rhun, not the least dismayed. "I say, that might be interesting. I should like to try it one day. But there's nothing like that to worry about. No one lives here. And they haven't for a long time."

"Hurry, then," Taran said, resolving never again to let Prince Rhun out of his sight. "We must join the others. We'll have long, hard riding before we catch up to them."

"Immediately!" said Rhun, who was wearing nothing but his shirt. "I shall get my things together."

Gurgi, meanwhile, had clambered down from the tree. His curiosity getting the better of his prudence, he loped across the clearing and thrust his head into the doorway, at last venturing inside with Rhun. Fflewddur and the impatient Taran followed

him.

It was, Taran saw, as the Prince had told them. A heavy layer of dust covered the wooden tables and benches. A spider had spun an enormous web in one corner, but even the web was deserted. On a broken hearthstone lay the charred remnants of a long-dead fire. Near the hearth, a number of large cookpots, dry and empty now, had been overturned. Earthen bowls and tall jars, shattered into fragments, were strewn about the floor. Through the holes in the roof the leaves of more than one autumn had fallen, nearly burying a stool whose legs had broken into splinters. The hut was silent; the noises of the forest did not enter. Taran stood uneasily while Prince Rhun fumbled with his gear.

Gurgi, fascinated by so many strange odds and ends, lost no time in poking through them. Suddenly he cried out in surprise. "Look, look!" he called, holding up a sheaf of tattered parchment.

Taran knelt beside Gurgi and examined the ragged bundle. The field mice, he realized, had discovered the packet long before. Many of the sheets had been gnawed away; others were rain sodden and blotted. The few undamaged pages were covered with cramped writing. Only at the bottom of the pile did Taran find pages in good repair. These had been carefully bound in leather to make a small tome, and their surface was clear and unmarked.

Prince Rhun, who still had not got around to buckling on his sword, came to peer over Taran's shoulder. "I say!" he cried. "What have you there? I can't guess what it is, but it looks interesting. And isn't that a handsome little book? I shouldn't mind having it to put down things I'm supposed to remember to do."

"Prince Rhun," Taran said, handing the undamaged volume to the Prince of Mona, who thrust it into his jacket, "believe me, if there's anything that might ever help you do anything, you're welcome to it." He went back to puzzling over the parchments. "Between the mice and the weather," he went on, "there's not much to make out of this scrawl. There seems to be no beginning or ending, but as far as I can tell, these are recipes for potions."

"Potions!" cried Fflewddur. "Great Belin, that's something we've little use for!"

Taran, nevertheless, continued to scan and sort the pages. "Wait, I think I've found the name of whoever wrote them. Glew, it looks like. And the potions, as it says here, are to"—his voice faltered and he turned anxiously to Fflewddur—"to make yourself grow bigger. What can this mean?"

"How's that?" asked the bard. "Bigger? Are you sure you haven't read it wrong?" He took the pages from Taran's hand and examined them carefully himself. When he had finished, he gave a low whistle.

"In my wanderings," said Fflewddur, "I've managed to learn a number of things, not least of which is don't meddle. I fear that's exactly what this fellow Glew did. Indeed, what he sought was a potion to make himself bigger and stronger. If those are Glew's boots over there," he added, pointing to the corner, "he surely needed one, for he must have been a little fellow."

Half hidden by leaves, a pair of well-worn boots lay on their side. They were hardly large enough to fit a child and seemed, to Taran, pitiful in their smallness and emptiness.

"He must have been painstaking," Fflewddur went on. "I'll say that much for him. He describes everything he did, and set down all his recipes, quite carefully and methodically. As for his ingredients," the bard said, making a sour face, "I should rather not think about them."

"I say," Prince Rhun eagerly interrupted, "perhaps we should try them ourselves. It would be interesting to see what happens."

"No, no!" Gurgi shouted. "Gurgi wants no tastings of nasty lotions and potions!"

"Nor do I," said Fflewddur. "And neither did Glew, for the matter of that. He had no wish to drink his concoctions until he had some hope they'd work— for which I can't blame him in the least. He went about it very cleverly.

"As I gather from what he's written down here," continued the bard, "he went out and trapped a mountain cat—a small one, I should think, since Glew himself was such a small person. He brought her back, put her in a cage, and fed her his potions as fast as he could cook them up."

"Poor creature," said Taran.

"Indeed," agreed the bard. "I shouldn't have liked to be in her place. Yet he must have grown fond enough of her to give her a name. Here, he's written it down. Llyan. Apart from feeding her those dreadful messes, I expect he didn't treat her badly. She might even have been company for him, living alone as he did.

"At last it happened," Fflewddur went on. "You can see by his writing how excited Glew must have been. Llyan began to grow. Glew mentions he was obliged to make a new cage for her. And still another. How pleased he must have been. I can easily imagine the little fellow chuckling and brewing away for all he was worth."

Fflewddur turned to the last page. "And, so it ends," he said, "where the mice have eaten the parchment. They've done away with Glew's last recipe. As for Glew and Llyan—they've vanished along with it."

Taran was silent looking at the empty boots and overturned cookpots. "Glew certainly is gone," he said thoughtfully, "but I have a feeling he didn't go far."

"How's that?" asked the bard. "Oh, I take your meaning," he said, shuddering. "Yes, it does look rather—shall I say, sudden? As I see Glew, he was a neat and orderly sort. He would hardly go off leaving his hut as it is now. Without his boots at that. Poor little fellow," he sighed. "It only proves the dangers of meddling. For all his pains, Glew must have got himself gobbled up. And if you ask me, the wisest thing for us is to leave immediately!"

79   Taran nodded and rose to his feet. As he did,

terrified whinnyings and the sound of galloping hooves filled the air. "The horses!" he cried, racing to the door.

Before he could reach it, the door burst from its hinges. Taran clutched at his sword and stumbled back into the hut as a huge shape leaped at him.

CHAPTER VII

The Lair of Llyan

Taran's blade went spinning from his grasp and he threw himself to the ground to escape the onslaught. In a powerful spring, the creature passed over his head. The great beast screamed with fury as the companions scattered in terror to all parts of the hut.

Amid the confusion of tumbling stools and benches, and as the dry leaves rose in a whirlwind, Taran saw that Fflewddur had jumped to a tabletop and, in so doing, had plunged into the spiderweb which now covered him from head to foot. Prince Rhun, having tried vainly to climb up the chimney, crouched in the ashes of the hearth. Gurgi had made himself as small as he could and had pressed into a corner, where he squealed and yelled, "Help, oh, help! Save Gurgi's poor tender head from pawings and clawings!"

"It's Llyan!" cried Taran.

"You can be sure it is!" Fflewddur shouted. "Now that I see her, I quite believe Glew was gobbled up and digested long ago."

A long, wavering growl rose from the creature's

throat and she hesitated a moment as if undecided where to attack. Taran, sitting up on the ground, saw for the first time what the ferocious animal looked like.

Though Glew had written of Llyan's growth, Taran had never imagined a mountain cat so big. The animal stood as tall as a horse but leaner and longer; her tail alone, thicker than Taran's arm, seemed to take up much of the room in the hut. Heavily and sleekly furred, the cat's body was golden-tawny, flecked with black and orange. Her belly was white with black splotches. Curling tufts sprouted from the tips of her ears, and shaggy handfuls of fur curved at her powerful jaws. Her long whiskers twitched; her baleful yellow eyes darted from one companion to another. Judging from the white points of her teeth, glittering as her lips drew back in a snarl, Taran was certain Llyan could gulp down anything that suited her fancy.

The giant cat swung her great head toward Taran and moved lithely across the ground. As she did, Fflewddur unsheathed his sword; cobwebs and all, he jumped from the table, shouted at the top of his voice, and brandished the weapon. In an instant Llyan spun around. The lash of her tail sent Taran headlong once more; even before Fflewddur could strike, Llyan's heavy paw flickered through the air. Its motion was too rapid for Taran's eyes to follow; he saw only the astonished bard's weapon fly up and clatter into the doorway, while Fflewddur himself went head over heels.

With a snort and what seemed a shrug of her rippling shoulders, Llyan turned again to Taran. She crouched, thrust out her neck, and her whiskers trembled as she padded closer to him. Taran, not daring to move a muscle, held his breath. Llyan circled him, making snuffling noises. From the corner of his eye, Taran glimpsed the bard trying to climb to his feet, and warned Fflewddur to stay still.

"She's more curious than angry," Taran whispered. "Otherwise, she would have clawed us to pieces by now. Don't move. She may go away."

"Glad to hear you say that," replied Fflewddur in a choked voice. "I'll remember it while I'm being gobbled up. It will be a consolation to me."

"I don't think she's hungry," said Taran. "If she's been out hunting during the night, she must have eaten her fill."

"So much the worse for us," said Fflewddur. "She'll keep us here until her appetite comes back. I'm sure this is the first time she's been lucky enough to have four dinners ready and waiting in her lair." He sighed and shook his head. "In my own realm I was always putting out scraps for birds and other creatures, but I never thought I'd see the day when I'd be putting *myself* out, if you take my meaning."

At last, Llyan settled herself across the doorway. She moistened a huge paw with her tongue and began passing it over her ear. Engrossed in her task, she seemed to have forgotten the companions were there. Despite his fear, Taran could not help staring at her in fascination. Power filled even Llyan's gentlest movements; beneath the golden fur, glowing in the sunlight from the open door, he could guess at her mighty muscles. Llyan, he was certain, could be swift as Melynlas. But he knew also she could be deadly; and, though she did not appear ill-disposed toward the companions, her mood might change at any instant. Taran cast about desperately for a way to freedom, or at least a means of regaining their weapons.

"Fflewddur," he whispered, "make a little noise, not too much but enough so that Llyan will look at you."

"How's that?" asked the bard, puzzled. "Look at me? She'll do that soon enough. I'm thankful she hasn't yet got around to it." However, he scraped his boots across the floor. Llyan immediately pricked up her ears and turned her eyes on the bard.

Crouching, Taran moved silently toward Llyan, his hand outstretched. His fingers cautiously reached for his sword which lay close to Llyan's paws. Quick as lightning, the mountain cat struck at him and he fell back. Had her claws been unsheathed, Taran realized with a sinking feeling, Llyan would have gained his head in addition to his weapon.

"No chance, my friend," said Fflewddur. "She's faster than any of us."

"We can be hindered no longer!" Taran cried. "Time is precious!"

"Oh, indeed it is," the bard answered, "and gets more precious the less of it we have. I'm beginning to envy Princess Eilonwy. Magg may be a foul, villainous spider and all such as that, but when it comes to teeth and claws—I should vastly prefer going against him instead of Llyan. 'No, no,'' he sighed, "I'm quite content to stretch my last moments as far as they'll reach.''

Taran in despair pressed his hands against his forehead. "Prince Rhun," he called softly after a moment, as Llyan began passing a paw over her whiskers, "stand up quietly. See if you can make your way to that broken corner of the hut. If so, climb out and run for your life."

The Prince of Mona nodded, but no sooner had he risen to his feet than Llyan growled a warning. Prince Rhun blinked and quickly sat down again. Llyan glared at the companions.

"Great Belin!" whispered Fflewddur. "Don't rouse her up any more. It will only bring on her appetite. She's not going to let us out of here, that's one thing sure."

"But we must escape," Taran urged. "What if we all rushed upon her once? One of us at least might get past."

Fflewddur shook his head. "After she'd settled with the rest of us," he answered, "she'd have no trouble catching up with that lone survivor. Let me think, let me think." Frowning, he reached behind him and unslung his harp. Llyan, still growling, watched intently, but made no further move.

"It always calms me," explained Fflewddur, putting the instrument against his shoulder and passing his hands over the harp strings. "I don't know whether it will stir up any ideas; but when I'm playing, at least things don't seem quite so dismal."

As a soft melody rose from the harp, Llyan began making a peculiar noise. "Great Belin," cried Fflewddur, stopping immediately, "I almost forgot about her! It may be calming for me, but who can tell what it might do to a mountain cat!"

Llyan now voiced a strange, pleading yowl. But, seeing Fflewddur about to sling the harp on his shoulder once again, her tone changed and sharpened. She growled menacingly.

"Fflewddur!" Taran whispered. "Play on!"

"You can't think she enjoys it," replied the bard. "I should find that hard to believe. Why, even human beings have been known to say hard words about my music. You can't expect a mountain cat to like it any better." Nevertheless, he plucked the strings once more.

This time, there was no doubt in Taran's mind that Llyan was fascinated by the harp. The great body of the cat slackened, her muscles seemed to uncoil, and Llyan blinked peacefully. To make certain, Taran asked Fflewddur to stop. As soon as the bard did so, Llyan turned restless. Her tail lashed and her whiskers trembled with what could only be vexation. As soon as the bard played again, Llyan put her head to one side, ears forward, and gazed fondly at him.

"Yes, yes!" Gurgi cried. "Do not leave off hummings and strummings!"

"Believe me," the bard answered fervently, "I haven't the slightest intention."

Llyan folded her paws under her deep, speckled chest and began making a sound like a swarm of droning bees. Her mouth curved in a smile and the tip of her tail moved gently to the music.

"That's the answer!" cried Fflewddur, springing to his feet. "Fly, friends, while she's quiet!" No sooner had he risen than Llyan, too, jumped up, furious, and the bard sank back, playing for dear life.

"Your music calms her," Taran cried in alarm, "but she still won't let us go."

"Not exactly," said the bard, passing his fingers rapidly across the strings. "I doubt if the rest of you will have any trouble. Alas," he added ruefully, "I fear *I'm* the one she wants to keep!"

CHAPTER VIII

The Harp of Fflewddur

Fly from here!" urged the bard, never ceasing to pluck his harp strings. "Begone! I've no idea how long she'll want to listen—or how long I can keep playing!"

"There must be another way," Taran cried. "We can't leave you."

"I like it no more than you do," replied the bard. "But this is your chance. You must take it now."

Taran hesitated. Fflewddur's face was grim and drawn, and he seemed already weary.

"Begone!" Fflewddur repeated. "I'll play as long as I can. By then, if she's decided not to gobble me, she may go out hunting. Don't worry. If the harp fails, I'll think of something else."

Sick at heart, Taran turned away. Llyan lay on her side across the threshold, one paw outstretched, the other gently curled against her tawny body. Her neck arched and her huge head turned toward Fflewddur. The fierce creature seemed altogether comfortable and peaceful. With yellow eyes half-closed, she watched only the bard as Taran stealthily moved to join Gurgi and Prince Rhun. Taran's sword remained with the other weapons beneath her paw, and he dared not attempt to snatch it away, fearful as he was of breaking the spell of Fflewddur's harp.

The fallen stones at the corner of the hut gave a narrow passage into the clearing. Taran motioned hurriedly for the Prince to go through. Gurgi followed on tiptoe, eyes wide with fright; he clutched his jaws in both hands to keep his teeth from chattering.

Taran still hung back, and turned once more to the bard, who gestured frantically.

"Out, out!" commanded Fflewddur. "I shall find you as soon as I can. Did I not promise you a new song? You shall hear it from my own lips. Until then— farewell!"

Fflewddur's tone and glance left no room for question. Taran flung himself past the stones. In another instant he was free of the hut.

As Taran feared, the horses had broken their tethers and fled at the sight of Llyan. Gurgi and Prince Rhun had crossed the clearing and vanished into the forest. Racing at top speed, Taran soon caught up with them. Rhun's pace had already begun to flag, his breathing was labored, and he looked as though his legs might give way at any moment. Taran and Gurgi caught the staggering Prince and bore him along as fast as they could.

For some while, the three struggled through the underbrush. The forest had begun to grow sparser and Taran caught sight of a broad meadow. At the edge of the flatland, he halted. Prince Rhun, he knew, had reached the end of his strength and he hoped only that they were a safe distance from Llyan.

The Prince of Mona gratefully dropped to the turf. "I shall be up and about in a moment," he feebly insisted. His face was pale and drawn beneath its coating of soot, yet he tried valiantly to assume his usual cheerful grin. "Amazing how running seems to tire one. I'll be glad when we find the Master of Horse and I can ride again."

Taran did not answer immediately but looked closely at Rhun. The Prince of Mona bowed his head.

"I can guess what you're thinking," Rhun said in a low voice. "If it hadn't been for me, you wouldn't be in this plight. And I'm afraid you're right. It's my fault things turned out as they did. I can only ask your forgiveness. I'm not the cleverest person in the world," Rhun added, smiling sadly. "Even my old nurse used to say I was all thumbs. But I hate being a blunderer. It's not what people expect of a Prince. I didn't ask to be born into the Royal House, *that* at least wasn't my doing. But, since I was, I—I want very much to be worthy of it."

"If you want to, then you shall." Taran answered, suddenly and strangely touched by the Prince of Mona's frankness, and not a little ashamed of his own unkind thoughts about Rhun. "I ask your own forgiveness. If I envied your rank, it was because I believed you held it as a lucky gift and took it for granted. You speak the truth. For a man to be worthy of any rank, he must strive first to be a man."

"Yes, that's what I mean," Rhun said eagerly. "That's why we must rejoin the Master of Horse as soon as we can. Don't you see? In this I'd hoped not to fail. I want—well—I want to be the one who finds Princess Eilonwy. After all, I'm to be betrothed to her."

Taran looked at him in astonishment. "How do you know this? I had thought only your parents . . ."

"Oh, there have been rumors around the castle," replied Rhun, "and I sometimes hear a little more than I'm supposed to. I knew there was a betrothal in the wind even before I was sent to bring Princess Eilonwy to Mona."

"Eilonwy's safe return is all that matters now," Taran began. He spoke slowly, knowing in his heart that he, no less than Rhun, yearned to be Eilonwy's rescuer. But he realized there was a decision he must face without flinching. "The searchers by this time are far distant," Taran said, each word costing him an effort, yet each word forcing him to a choice as painful as it was clear. "Without horses, we cannot hope to reach them. Continuing our own search on foot would be too hard and too dangerous. We have only one path to follow: the one that will lead us back to Dinas Rhydnant."

"No, no!" Rhun cried. "I don't care about the danger. I must find Eilonwy."

"Prince Rhun," Taran said gently, "I must also tell you this. Your father asked for my oath, and I have given it, to keep you from harm."

Rhun's face fell. "I might have guessed as

much. Certainly I knew from the beginning, no matter what my father said about putting me in command, I wasn't really leading. No more than I am now. I understand. I'm under your orders. Whatever's to be done, you are the one to decide."

"There are others who can finish the task," Taran said. "As for us . . ."

"See with lookings!" burst out Gurgi, who had been crouching near a fallen ash tree. "See, coming with chasings and racings!" He waved his arms excitedly and pointed to a low ridge. Taran made out a figure running at top speed.

His harp bouncing at his shoulder, his cloak rolled up and clutched under one arm, and his lanky legs pumping for all they were worth, the bard dashed down the slope. He flung himself to the ground and mopped his streaming face.

"Great Belin!" Fflewddur gasped. "I'm glad to see all of you again." From his cloak he drew out the lost swords and handed them to the companions. "And I think we shall all be glad to see these."

"Are you wounded?" Taran asked. "How did you escape? How did you find us?"

Still puffing, the bard raised a hand. "Give me a moment to catch my breath, for I lost it somewhere along the way. Wounded? Well, yes, in a manner of speaking," he added, glancing at his blistered fingers. "But I had no trouble finding you. Rhun must have carried off all the ashes in Glew's fireplace. I could hardly miss the trail.

"As for Llyan," Fflewddur went on, "the bards

will sing of that, you can be sure. I must have played, sung, whistled, and hummed everything I ever knew, and twice over. I was sure I'd have to keep plucking and strumming for the rest of my life, however short that might be. Recall my plight!" he cried, leaping to his feet. "Alone with a ferocious monster. Bard against beast! Beast against bard!"

"You slew her," Taran exclaimed. "A bold stroke—though a pity, for she was beautiful in her way."

"Ah—well, the truth of it is," Fflewddur said hastily, for the harp strings had tensed as though they might all break at once, "she finally went to sleep. I snatched up our swords and ran for dear life."

Fflewddur sank back to the turf and immediately began munching the food Gurgi had offered him.

"But I shouldn't vouch for Llyan's temper when she wakens," the bard continued. "She's bound to come after me. These mountain cats are trackers born; and since Llyan's ten times bigger than an ordinary creature, she's surely ten times more cunning. She'll not give up easily. I have the feeling her patience is as long as her tail. But I'm surprised you've not gone farther. I thought you'd be well on your way to join the search."

Taran shook his head. He told the bard of the decision to return to Dinas Rhydnant.

"I suppose it's the best thing to do," Fflewddur reluctantly agreed. "Especially now, when Llyan may be prowling."

Taran scanned the hills for the easiest and safest path to follow. He caught his breath. A dark shape sped high above. It veered, circled, then drove directly toward him.

"It's Kaw!" Taran ran ahead and held out his arms. The crow dropped swiftly and lighted on Taran's outstretched wrist. The bird showed signs of grueling flight; his feathers were askew and he looked like a bundle of rags, but he clacked his beak and jabbered excitedly.

"Eilonwy!" Kaw croaked. "Eilonwy!"

CHAPTER IX

The Luck of Rhun

He's found her!" Taran shouted, as the companions pressed around the frantic crow. "Where has Magg taken her?"

"Alaw!" croaked Kaw. "Alaw!"

"The river!" Taran exclaimed. "How far is it?"

"Close! Close!" replied Kaw.

"No question of going back to Dinas Rhydnant now," cried Prince Rhun. "Magg's in our hands. We'll have the Princess back again in no time at all."

"If Llyan doesn't have us in her paws first," muttered Fflewddur. He turned to Taran. "Can Kaw bear word to the Master of Horse? I don't mind telling you I should feel safer with a few warriors behind me."

"We dare not lose time," Taran answered. "Prince Rhun is right. We must act now or Magg will slip through our fingers. Quickly, old friend," he said to Kaw, urging the crow aloft, "guide us to the Alaw."

They set off in haste. The crow fluttered from one tree to the next, jabbering impatiently until the companions drew closer. Then, launching himself once more into the air, Kaw streaked onward in the direction he wished them to follow. The crow, Taran knew, was doing his best to bring them as quickly as possible out of the hills; but many times the forest and underbrush formed such a tangled barrier the companions were forced to draw their swords and hack their way through.

Their path did not ease until well past midday, when Kaw led them across a low, rolling plain which soon fell into pebbly ravines. The turf was short and stubbly, with many splotches of bare ground where chalk-white boulders were strewn like giant hailstones.

"With all of Rhuddlum's warriors combing Mona," Fflewddur cried angrily, as they began the descent toward the river, "how has that spider managed to escape us for so long?"

"Magg has been more cunning than we thought," Taran said bitterly. "I'm sure he took Eilonwy into the Hills of Parys. But he must have hidden away, without moving until he knew the search had swept beyond him."

"The villain!" Fflewddur snorted. "So it must have been. While we all went tracking farther and farther away from the castle, that foul Magg waited at his ease until we'd gone so far ahead that he was behind us! No matter. We'll soon have him by the heels and he'll pay for that trick!"

Kaw, circling in great loops above the companions, had grown more agitated and began a raucous croaking. Taran caught a glimpse of the Alaw flashing below. Kaw, in a burst of speed, flew directly toward it. With Prince Rhun gasping and puffing behind them, the companions ran down the slope. Kaw, lighting on a branch, madly flapped his wings.

Taran's heart sank. There was no trace of Eilonwy or Magg. In another moment he dropped to one knee. Fflewddur!" he shouted. "Quickly! Here are hoof prints. Two horses." He followed the trail for a few paces, then halted, puzzled.

"See this," he said to the bard and Gurgi, who had come up beside him. "The tracks follow different paths. I don't understand what could have happened. Prince Rhun," he called, "can you see anything of the steeds?"

No answer came from the Prince of Mona. Taran leaped to his feet and spun about. "Rhun!" he cried. But there was no sign whatever of the Prince. "He's wandered off again!" Taran shouted furiously. "Feckless dolt! Where has he gone?"

Calling anxiously for Rhun, the three raced on to the riverbank. Taran was about to set off alone to seek him when the Prince of Mona appeared from a stand of willows.

"Hullo, hullo!" Rhun hurried forward, beaming delightedly. Before the relieved but angry Taran could take him to task, the Prince called out, "Look at this! Amazing! Really astonishing!"

Prince Rhun held out his hand. In it lay Eilonwy's bauble.

His heart pounding, Taran stared at the golden sphere. "Where did you find this?"

"Why, over there," answered Rhun, pointing to a moss-covered rock. "While you were looking at hoof prints, I thought I might go and search somewhere else to save us time. And this is what I found." He handed the bauble to Taran, who carefully tucked it into his jacket.

"He's led us to fresh tracks," said Fflewddur, studying the grass. "Something fairly large and flat has been dragged along here." He scratched his chin thoughtfully. "I wonder—a boat? Could it be? Did that sneering spider have one ready and waiting? I shouldn't be surprised if he had planned it all before Eilonwy reached Mona."

Taran strode down the bank. "I see footprints," he called. "The ground is badly torn. Eilonwy must have struggled with him—yes, right there. And there she would have dropped the bauble." In dismay he looked at the wide, rapid-flowing Alaw. "You have read the signs well, Fflewddur," he said. "Magg had a boat here. He set loose the horses and let them run as they pleased."

Taran stood a moment watching the turbulent water, then drew his sword. "Come, lend me a hand," he called to Gurgi and the bard, and ran to the willows.

"I say, what have you in mind?" cried Rhun, as Taran chopped hastily at the lower branches. "Making a fire? There's hardly any need."

"We can build a raft," replied Taran, throwing the cut branches on the ground. "The river has helped Magg. Now it shall help us."

The companions ripped vines from the tree trunks and lashed the cut branches together, lengthening the makeshift cords with strips torn from their own garments. Ungainly though it was, and looking more like a bundle of kindling wood, the raft was soon ready. But no sooner had Taran begun tying the last knots in the tangle of vines and rags when Gurgi shrieked in fear. Taran leaped to his feet and spun around as Gurgi gestured wildly toward the trees farther up the riverbank.

Llyan had burst from the woods. The great tawny mountain cat halted for an instant, one paw raised, her tail lashing, her eyes blazing at the companions, who fell back in terror.

"The raft!" Taran shouted. "Into the river with it!" He seized one end of the clumsy craft and struggled to haul it to the water. Still yelling, Gurgi ran to aid him. Prince Rhun toiled as best he could to help. The bard had already splashed into the stream, where he stood hip-deep in the current and heaved at the branches.

Llyan's tufted ears cupped forward and her whiskers twitched as her glance fell on the bard. From her throat arose not a savage roar but a bell-like, questioning cry. Eyes shining with a strange glow, she loped forward on huge padded paws. Purring loudly, the mountain cat made straight for the frantic bard.

"Great Belin!" cried Fflewddur. "She wants me back again!"

It was then that Kaw, perched on a low branch, beat his wings and launched himself against Llyan.

Squawking and croaking at the top of his voice, the crow swooped down on the astonished beast. Llyan stopped in her tracks and roared angrily. Flying at full speed, Kaw passed within a hair's breadth of Llyan's mighty head, striking out with his wings and pecking at her with his sharp beak.

Taken by surprise, Llyan fell back on her haunches and turned to face the crow. Kaw veered in a tight circle and swooped again. Llyan sprang into the air, claws unsheathed and slashing. Taran cried in dismay as a cloud of feathers floated downward, but an instant later he saw the crow still aloft and plunging again toward Llyan. Dancing in front of her like a large black hornet, Kaw jabbered impudently as though daring the beast to catch him, flapped his wings in her face, and sped away once more. At his next dive, which brought him so close that Llyan's teeth snapped shut on one of his tail feathers, Kaw seized and tweaked a curling whisker.

Yowling furiously, forgetting the bard and the struggling companions, Llyan raced after the crow who flapped from the riverbank into the woods. Llyan followed, and her roars echoed among the trees.

With a final heave, the companions flung the raft into the river and scrambled aboard. The current snatched and spun the craft, nearly capsizing it before Taran could thrust a pole into the water. Fflewddur and Gurgi fended the raft off a threatening boulder. Prince Rhun, drenched to the skin, paddled desperately with his hands. In another moment the

raft righted itself and the companions skimmed rapidly downstream.

Fflewddur, whose face had turned deathly
pale, gave a sigh of relief. "I feared she had me for
sure! Believe me, I couldn't stand another bout of
harping like the last one! I hope Kaw fares well," he
added anxiously.

"Kaw will find us again," Taran assured him.
"He's clever enough to stay out of Llyan's reach until
he knows we're safe. If she keeps chasing him, I'm
certain she'll have the worst of the battle."

Fflewddur nodded, then turned and glanced
back over his shoulder. "In a way," he said, with a
note of regret in his voice, "it's the first time my music
has really been—ah—in a manner of speaking, sought
after. In this case, if it weren't so dangerous, I should
call it downright complimentary!"

"I say," called Prince Rhun, crouching at the
front of the raft, "I don't mean to complain after all
the work you've done, but I think something's breaking loose."

Taran, busy steering, glanced down in alarm.
The hurriedly knotted vines had begun to give way.
The raft shuddered in the swift current. With the
pole, Taran thrust deeply for the river bottom, seeking
to bring the raft to a halt. The current bore it onward
and the branches bent and twisted as the water
poured through the gaps. One of the vines parted, a
branch ripped free, then another. Throwing aside the
useless pole, Taran shouted for the companions to

jump clear. Seizing Prince Rhun by the jacket, he sprang into the river.

As the water closed over his head, Prince Rhun kicked and struggled wildly. Taran tightened his grasp on the floundering Prince and fought his way to the surface. With a free hand he clung to a boulder and gained a foothold among the shifting stones. Heaving with all his strength, he dragged Rhun ashore and flung him to the bank.

Gurgi and Fflewddur had managed to catch hold of what remained of the raft and were hauling it into the shallows. Prince Rhun sat up and looked around.

"That's the closest I've ever been to drowning," he gasped. "I've often wondered what it was like, though now I don't think I'd care to know."

"Drowning?" said Fflewddur, staring at the wreckage of the craft. "Worse than that! All our labor has gone for naught."

Taran rose wearily to his feet. "Most of the branches can be used. We'll cut more vines and start again."

The discouraged companions turned to the task of repairing the raft, now strewn in pieces along the bank. The work went more slowly than before, for the trees grew sparser here and vines were scarce.

The Prince of Mona had made his way to a clump of osiers, and Taran glimpsed him tugging away, trying to uproot them. The next instant, Rhun was no longer in sight.

With a shout of alarm, Taran dropped his armload of vines and ran toward the spot, calling Rhun's name.

The bard looked up. "Not again!" he cried. "If there were a field with one stone he'd trip over it! A Fflam is patient, but there are limits!" Nevertheless, he hurried to join Taran, who was already kneeling among the osiers.

At the spot where Rhun had been standing was a gaping hole. The Prince of Mona had vanished.

CHAPTER X

The Cavern

eedless of Fflewddur's warning shout, Taran leaped into the pit and slid quickly past a mesh of torn roots. The hole widened a little, then dropped straight. Calling for the bard to lower a length of vine, he let himself fall, then scrambled to his feet and struggled to lift up the unconscious Rhun, who was bleeding heavily from a gash at the side of his head.

The end of the vine dangled from above. Taran seized and lashed it securely under the Prince's arms, shouting for Fflewddur and Gurgi to pull him up. The vine tautened, strained—and snapped. Earth and stones showered from the raw sides of the hole.

"Beware!" Taran cried. "The ground is giving way!"

"Afraid you're right," Fflewddur called back. "In that case, I think we'd better give you a hand from down there."

Taran saw the soles of Fflewddur's boots plunge toward him. The bard landed with a grunt, and Gurgi, whose hair looked as though it had scraped away most of the dirt from the hole, tumbled after.

Prince Rhun's eyelids fluttered. "Hullo, hullo!" he murmured. "What happened? Those roots were surprisingly deep!"

"The land must be eaten away along the river-bank," Taran said. "When you pulled, the strain and weight opened up this hole. Never fear," he added quickly, "we'll soon have you out. Help us to turn you. Can you move at all?"

The Prince nodded, gritted his teeth, and, with the companions lifting him, began painfully clambering up the side of the pit. But he had gone no more than halfway when he lost his handhold. Taran scrambled to block his fall. Rhun clutched wildly at a root and hung poised a moment in mid-air.

The root tore free and Rhun plummeted downward. The wall of earth rumbled as the pit collapsed around them. Taran flung up his arms against the rush of soil and shale. He was thrown down, the ground cracked at his feet, fell away, and left him spinning in nothingness.

A violent shock stunned him. Loose earth filled his nose and mouth. Lungs bursting, he fought against the weight pressing the life from him. It was only then he realized he had stopped falling. His head still reeled, but he twisted and clawed his way through dirt and pebbles. He heaved himself upward, breathing once again.

Gasping and trembling, he dropped at full length on a sloping, rocky floor, in darkness so deep it seemed to suffocate him. At last regaining strength enough to lift his head, he tried vainly to peer through the shadows that filled his eyes. He called to the companions, but no answer came. His voice rang with a strange, hollow echo. In despair, he shouted once more.

"Hullo, hullo!" called another voice.

"Prince Rhun!" Taran cried. "Where are you? Are you safe?"

"I don't know," answered the Prince. "If I could see better, I could tell you better."

Raising himself to hands and knees, Taran crawled forward. His groping fingers met a shaggy mass that stirred and whimpered.

"Terrible, oh terrible!" moaned Gurgi. "Rumblings and crumblings fling poor Gurgi into fearsome blackness. He cannot see!"

"Great Belin," came Fflewddur's voice out of the dark, "I'm delighted to hear that. For a moment I thought I'd been struck blind. I swear I can see more with my eyes shut!"

Ordering Gurgi to hang on to his belt, Taran crept in the direction of the bard's voice. Soon the companions had found each other again, and also Prince Rhun who had managed to drag himself toward them.

"Fflewddur," Taran said in an anxious voice, "I fear the landslide has blocked the pit. Dare we try to dig our way out?"

"I don't think it's so much a question of digging as it is of finding, if you take my meaning," replied the bard. "Whether we can burrow through all that dirt is, to say the least of it, highly doubtful.

Even a mole would have trouble, though *I'm* willing to give it a try. A Fflam is undaunted! But," he added, "without a light to guide us, we shall spend the rest of our days looking for the right spot to dig."

Taran nodded and knitted his brows. "It's true. Light is as precious to us as air." He turned to Gurgi. "Try to use your flints. We have no tinder here, but if I can catch the spark in my cloak it may be enough to set it alight." He heard rustling, slapping sounds, as though Gurgi were searching himself all over, and then a dismal wail.

"Fire stones are gone!" Gurgi moaned. "Wretched Gurgi cannot make bright blazing! He has lost them, oh misery and sorrow! Gurgi will go alone to seek them."

Taran patted the creature's shoulder. "Stay with us here," he said. "I value your life more than fire stones. We shall find some other way. Wait!" he cried. "Eilonwy's bauble! If only it will light for us!"

Quickly he thrust into his jacket and drew out the sphere. For a moment he held it covered in his hands, fearing disappointment should the bauble fail to glow.

Holding his breath, he slowly moved a hand away. The golden sphere lay cupped in his palm; he could feel its smooth, cool surface and its weight, which was somehow not weight at all. He sensed the eyes of the companions on him and could guess at their hopeful glances. But the darkness pressed heavier and more stifling than ever. The bauble gave not the slightest glimmer.

"I cannot do it," Taran murmured. "I fear it is not given to an Assistant Pig-Keeper to command such a thing of beauty and enchantment."

"No sense in my trying," said Prince Rhun. "I know I can't make it work. The very first time I held it, the thing blinked out the moment it was in my hands. Surprising! The Princess Eilonwy could light it so easily."

Taran groped toward Fflewddur and put the sphere into his hand. "You know the lore of the bards and the ways of enchantments," he urged. "Perhaps it will obey you. Try, Fflewddur. Our lives depend on it."

"Yes, well," replied Fflewddur, "I must admit I have no great skill in these things. The true lore of the bards, sorry to say, has always been a little beyond me. There's simply too much to know and I could never squeeze more than a drop or two into my head. But—a Fflam is willing!"

Moments passed, then Taran heard Fflewddur sigh with discouragement. "Can't get the hang of it," muttered the bard. "I even tried rapping it on the ground, but that doesn't do either. Here, let our friend Gurgi have a go at it."

"Woe and sorrow!" moaned Gurgi, after the bard had passed the sphere to him and he had held it for a while. "Even with teasings and squeezings, even with battings and pattings, unhappy Gurgi cannot bring golden winkings!"

"A Fflam never despairs!" cried Fflewddur. "But," he added dolefully, "I'm coming rapidly to believe this pit will be our grave, without even a decent mound to mark the spot. A Fflam is cheerful—but this is a disheartening situation, no matter how you look at it."

Gurgi silently gave the bauble back to Taran who, heavy-hearted, cupped it in his hands again. With yearning now he held it, and his mind turned from his own plight to thoughts of Eilonwy. He saw her face and once more heard her gay laughter ring clearer than the notes of Fflewddur's harp. He smiled to himself, even as he recalled her chattering and her sharp words.

He was about to return the bauble to his jacket, but stopped short and stared at his hand. A point of light had begun to flicker in the depths of the sphere. As he watched, not daring to breathe, it blossomed and shimmered.

Taran sprang to his feet with a cry not of triumph but of wonder. Golden beams shone around him faintly but steadily. Trembling, he raised the sphere high above his head.

"Kind master saves us!" cried Gurgi. "Yes, yes! He takes us from loomings and gloomings! Joy and happiness! Fearful darkness is gone! Gurgi can see again!"

"Amazing!" cried Prince Rhun. "Astonishing! Look at this cave! I never knew we had such a place on Mona!"

Again Taran cried out in wonder. Until now, he had believed they had fallen into something like a large burrow. The glow of Eilonwy's bauble showed they had come, instead, to the edge of an enormous cavern. It stretched before them like a forest after an ice storm. Columns of stone rose like the trunks of trees and arched to the ceiling where stone icicles clung. Along the shadowy walls, huge outcroppings sprang like hawthorn blossoms and glittered in the bauble's golden rays. Threads of scarlet and vivid green twisted through luminous shafts of rock. White tendrils of crystal curled along jagged walls gleaming with rivulets of water. Still other chambers lay beyond this one, and Taran caught sight of wide pools, flat and glistening as mirrors. Some gave a dull, greenish glow, others a pale blue.

"What have we found?" Taran whispered. "Can this be a part of the Fair Folk's realm?"

Fflewddur shook his head. "The Fair Folk surely have tunnels and caves where you'd least expect them, but I doubt this is one. There's no sign of life at all."

Gurgi did not speak, but stared with round eyes at the cavern. Prince Rhun, an expression of delight on his face, stepped ahead. "I say, this really is surprising!" he said. "I shall have to tell my father about this and see if he won't open it up to visitors. It would be a shame to keep it hidden away."

"It is a place of great beauty," Taran said in a hushed voice.

"And a deadly place for us," replied Fflewddur. "A Fflam enjoys the scenery—that's one advantage of being a wandering bard—but from the—ah—*outside*, if I make myself clear, which I believe is where we should put ourselves as quickly as we can."

The companions retraced their steps to where the landslide had carried them. As Taran had feared, the light of the golden ball showed that digging a passage would be vain, for heavy boulders filled the pit, blocking it entirely. While Prince Rhun rested on one of the table-like stones, and Gurgi delved into his wallet for food, Taran and Fflewddur spoke hastily between themselves.

"We must find another passage," Taran said. "King Rhuddlum and his men will never reach Eilonwy now. We are the only ones who know the direction Magg has taken."

"All too true," Fflewddur glumly replied. "Yet I fear that knowledge is going to stay locked up with us here. Achren herself couldn't have thrown us into a stronger prison.

"There are surely other ways in and out," the bard went on, "but these caverns can stretch who knows how far. Underground, they may be enormous —and the entry no bigger than a rabbit hole."

Nevertheless, they agreed they had no choice but to continue into the cavern and seek a passage leading them above ground. Keeping the Prince of Mona protectively between them, Taran and the bard set off through the forest of stone, with Gurgi trotting behind and clutching Taran's belt.

Without warning Prince Rhun suddenly cupped his hands around his mouth and shouted,

"Hullo! Hullo!" at the top of his voice. "Anyone here? Hullo!"

"Rhun!" Taran cried. "Be silent! You will bring more danger on us."

"I should hardly think so," answered Rhun innocently. "It seems to me that finding someone or something is better than finding nothing at all."

"And risk our necks doing so?" Taran retorted.

He halted until the echoes had died away. No further sound came from the reaches of the cavern, and Taran warily beckoned the companions forward.

The ground dipped and they found themselves amid stones that jutted like huge teeth from the ground. Farther on the cavern floor rolled and twisted in high waves and deep valleys, as though a stormy sea had been frozen motionless. Another chamber held massive piles of rock and tall mounds that had taken the fanciful shapes of unmoving clouds.

Here the toiling companions rested a moment, for the path had narrowed and grown more difficult. The air was heavy, stagnant as swamp water, and chilled them to the bone. Taran urged them to their feet once again, anxious to find a tunnel leading upward, but fearing more and more that their search would be long and painful. A glance at the bard's face told Taran that Fflewddur shared his fears.

"I say, there's an odd thing," called Rhun, pointing to a tumble of rock.

It was, indeed, one of the strangest shapes Taran had seen in the cavern, for it looked like a hen's egg sticking halfway out of a nest. The stone was white, smooth, and somewhat pointed at the top, crusted here and there with patches of lichen, and stood nearly as tall as Taran himself. What at first resembled a nest was a tangled, discolored fringe of coarse strands that seemed to balance on the edge of a sharp drop.

"Amazing!" called Rhun, who had insisted on striding closer to peer at it. "This isn't a rock at all!" He turned in surprise to the companions. "This is un-believable, but it's almost like . . ."

Taran seized the astonished Rhun and dragged him backward so abruptly the Prince nearly went head over heels. Gurgi yelped in terror. The shape had begun to move.

Two colorless eyes appeared, in a face pale as a dead fish; the eyebrows glittered with flecks of crystal; moss and mold edged the long, flapping ears and spread over the beard that sprouted below a lumpy nose.

Swords drawn, the companions huddled against the jagged wall. The huge head continued to rise and Taran saw it wobble on a skinny neck. A choking noise bubbled in the creature's throat as it cried, "Puny things! Tremble before me! Tremble, I tell you! I am Glew! I am Glew!"

CHAPTER XI

King of the Stones

urgi flung himself to the ground, covered his head with his hands, and whimpered piteously. The creature threw a long, spindly leg over the ledge and began slowly drawing himself upright. He was more than thrice as tall as Taran, and his flabby arms dangled below a pair of knobby, moss-covered knees. With a lopsided gait he shambled toward the companions.

"Glew!" Taran gasped. "But I was sure . . ."

"It can't be," whispered Fflewddur. "Impossible! Not little Glew! Or if it is, I certainly got the wrong impression of him."

"Tremble!" the quavering voice cried again. "You shall tremble!"

"Great Belin!" muttered the bard, who was indeed shaking so much he had almost dropped his blade, "I don't need to be told!"

The giant bent, shaded his white eyes against the light of the bauble, and peered at the companions. "Are you *really* trembling?" he asked in an anxious voice. "You're not doing it just to be obliging?"

Gurgi, meantime, had ventured to lift his hands from his face, but the sight of the creature towering above him made him clap them back again and set him to wailing louder than ever. Prince Rhun, however, recovering from his first shock, studied the monster with great curiosity. "I say, this is the first I've seen anyone with toadstools growing in his beard," he remarked. "Did he do it on purpose or did it just happen that way?"

"If that's the Glew we know," said the bard, "he's changed remarkably."

The giant's pale eyes widened. What would have been a smile on a face of ordinary size became a grin that stretched longer than Taran's arm. Glew blinked and stooped closer.

"You've heard of me then?" he asked eagerly.

"Indeed we have," put in Rhun. "It's amazing, but we thought Llyan . . ."

"Prince Rhun!" Taran warned.

Glew, for the moment, seemed to have no wish to harm them. Instead, evidently pleased by the consternation he had wrought among the companions, he was looking down at them with an expression of satisfaction all the more intense because it was so large. But until he had learned more of this strange creature, Taran had deemed it wiser to say nothing of their search.

"Llyan?" Glew quickly asked. "What do you know of Llyan?"

Since Rhun had already spoken, Taran had no choice but to admit the companions had stumbled upon Glew's hut. Disclosing no more than he had to, Taran told of finding the recipes for the potions. Whether Glew would take kindly to strangers rummaging among his possessions, Taran did not know; to his relief, the giant showed less concern about that than he did for the fate of the mountain cat.

"Oh, Llyan!" cried Glew. "If only she were here. Anything to keep me company!" At this he buried his face in his hands and the cavern echoed with his sobs.

"Now, now," said Fflewddur, "don't take on so. You're lucky you weren't gobbled up."

"Gobbled?" sniffed Glew, raising his head. "Better if I had been! Any doom rather than this miserable cavern. There's bats, you know. They've always terrified me, swooping and squeaking in that nasty way they have. Crawly white worms come popping their heads out of the rocks and stare at you. And spidery things! And things that are just—just things! They're the worst. It's enough to curdle your blood, I tell you! The other day, if I may call it day for all the difference it makes down here . . ."

The giant bent forward. His voice dropped to a roaring whisper, and he appeared eager to recount these happenings at great length.

"Glew," Taran interrupted, "we pity your plight, but I beg you, show us a way out of the cavern."

Glew rocked his huge, scraggly head from side to side. "Way out? I've never stopped looking for one. There isn't any. Not for me, at least."

"There must be," insisted Taran. "How did

you find your way into the cave in the first place? Please, show us."

"Find my way?" replied Glew. "I should hardly call it a question of finding. It was Llyan's fault. If only she hadn't broken from her cage the one time my potion was working so well. She chased me out of my hut. Ungrateful of her, but I forgive her. I still had the flask in my hand. Oh, how I wish I'd thrown the wretched potion away! I ran as fast as I could, with Llyan after me." Glew patted his forehead with a trembling hand and blinked sorrowfully. "I've never run so fast and so far in my life," he said. "I still dream of it, when I'm not dreaming of worse. Finally, I found a cave and into it I went.

"I hadn't a moment to spare," continued Glew, sighing heavily. "I swallowed the potion. Now that I've had time to think it over, I realize I shouldn't have. But it had made Llyan so much bigger, I thought it would do the same for me, so I might have a chance against her. And so it did," he added. "In fact, it worked so quickly I nearly broke my crown on the ceiling of the cave. And I kept on growing. I had to squeeze along as fast as I could, going farther and farther downward always looking for bigger chambers, until I ended here. By then, alas, no passage was wide enough to let me out.

"I've thought a great deal about it since that unhappy day. I often look back on it," Glew went on. He half closed his eyes and peered into the distance, lost in his own recollections. "I wonder now," he murmured, "I wonder now if . . ."

"Fflewddur," Taran whispered in the bard's

ear, "is there no way we can make him stop talking and show us one of the passages? Or should we try to slip by him and find it ourselves?"

"I don't know," answered Fflewddur. "From all the giants I've seen—yes, well, the truth of it is I've never seen any myself, though I've heard enough of them. Glew seems rather, how shall I say it, small! I don't know if I'm making myself clear, but he was a feeble little fellow to begin with and now he's a feeble little giant! And very likely a coward. I'm sure we could fight him, if we could *reach* him. Our biggest risk would be getting stepped on and squashed."

"I'm truly sorry for him," Taran began, "but I don't know how we can help him, and we dare not delay our search."

"You're not listening!" cried Glew, who had been talking on at some length before realizing he was talking mainly to himself. "Yes, it's the same thing all over again," he sobbed. "Even if I'm a giant, no one pays me any mind! Oh, I can tell you there are giants that would crack your bones and squeeze you until your eyes popped. You'd listen to them, you can be sure. But not Glew! Oh, it makes no difference about *him*, giant or no! Glew the giant, mewed up in a wretched cave and who's to care? Who's even to see?"

"Now look here," answered Fflewddur with some impatience, for the giant had begun to sob and splash the companions with tears, "you've only yourself to blame if you've put yourself into a stew. You meddled, and as I've said time and again, it leads to sad results."

"I didn't want to be a giant," protested Glew, "not at first anyway. I thought, once, I should be a famous warrior. I joined the host of Lord Goryon when he marched against Lord Gast. But I couldn't stand the sight of blood. It turned me green, green as grass. And those battles! Enough to make your head swim! All that clashing and smiting! The din alone is more than flesh can bear! No, no, it was absolutely out of the question."

"A warrior's life is one of hardship," Taran said, "and it takes a stout heart to follow it. Surely there were other means to make a name for yourself."

"I thought, then, I might become a bard," Glew went on. "It turned out as badly. The knowledge you must gain, the lore to be learned. . . ."

"I'm with you there, old fellow," murmured Fflewddur, with a sigh of regret. "I had rather the same experience."

"It wasn't the years of study," explained Glew in a voice that would have been forlorn had it not been so loud. "I know I could have learned if I'd taken the time. No, it was my feet. I couldn't bear all the tramping and wandering around from one end of Prydain to the other. And always sleeping in a different place. And the change of water. And the harp rubbing blisters on your shoulder. . . ."

"We grieve for you," interrupted Taran, shifting restlessly, "but we cannot tarry here."

Glew had crouched down in front of the companions and Taran tried desperately to think of the best means of getting past him.

"Please, please don't go!" cried Glew, as if reading Taran's thoughts, his eyes blinking frantically. "Not yet! I'll show you a passage in a moment, I promise."

"Yes, yes!" shouted Gurgi, at last able to bring himself to open his eyes and clamber to his feet. "Gurgi does not like caverns. And his poor tender head is filled with soundings and poundings!"

"It was then I decided to become a hero," Glew eagerly went on, ignoring the impatience of the companions, "to go about slaying dragons and such. But you can't imagine how difficult it is. Why, even *finding* a dragon is almost impossible! But I discovered one in Cantrev Mawr.

"It was a small dragon," admitted Glew. "About the size of a weasel. The cottagers had it penned up in a rabbit hutch and the children used to go and look at it when they'd nothing else to do. But it was a dragon nevertheless. I would have slain it," he added, with a huge, rattling sigh. "I tried. But the vicious thing bit me. I still carry the marks."

Taran tightened his grip on his sword. "Glew," he said firmly, "I beg you once again to show us the passage. If you will not . . ."

"Then I thought I might become a king," Glew said hurriedly, before Taran could finish. "I thought if I could wed a princess—but no, they turned me away at the castle gate.

"What else could I do?" moaned Glew, shaking his head miserably. "What was left for me but to try enchantments? At last I came upon a wizard who claimed to have a book of spells in his possession. He wouldn't tell me how it had fallen into his hands, but he assured me the magic it held was most powerful. It had once belonged to the House of Llyr."

Taran caught his breath at these words. "Eilonwy is a Princess of the House of Llyr," he whispered to the bard. "What tale is Glew telling us? Is he speaking the truth?"

"It had come," Glew went on, "from Caer Colur itself. Naturally, I . . ."

"Glew, tell me quickly," Taran cried, "what is Caer Colur? What has it to do with the House of Llyr?"

"Why, everything," replied Glew, as though surprised at Taran's asking. "Caer Colur is the ancient seat of the House of Llyr. I should think everyone would know that. A very treasurehouse of charms and enchantments. Oh my, yes. So, as I was saying, naturally I believed I had at last found something to help me. The wizard was eager to be rid of the book, as eager as I was to have it."

Taran's hands had suddenly begun to tremble. "Where is Caer Colur?" he asked. "How can we find it?"

"Find it?" said Glew. "I don't know if there's much left of it to find. They say the castle has been in ruins for years. Bewitched, too, as you might expect. And you should have some hard rowing to do."

"Rowing overland?" said Fflewddur. "Don't ask us to believe that."

"Rowing," repeated Glew, nodding sorrowfully. "Long ago, Caer Colur was part of Mona. But it broke from the mainland during a flood. Now it's no more than a speck of island. Be that as it may," Glew went on, "I took all the little treasure I had managed to save . . . ."

"Where is the island?" Taran pressed. "Glew, you must tell us. It is important for us to know."

"At the mouth of the Alaw," replied Glew, with a certain vexation at being interrupted once more. "But that has nothing to do with what happened to me. You see, the wizard . . . ."

Taran's mind raced. Magg had taken Eilonwy to the Alaw. He had needed a boat. Was Eilonwy's ancestral home his destination? His glance met Fflewddur's, and the bard's expression showed he had been following the same thought.

". . . the wizard," Glew continued, "was in such haste that I had no chance to see the book. Until it was too late. He had cheated me. It was a book—a book of nothing! Of empty pages!"

"Amazing!" cried Prince Rhun. "The very book we found!"

"Worthless," sighed Glew, "but since you found it, you may keep it. It's yours. A gift. Something to remember me by. So you won't forget poor Glew."

"Small chance of that," muttered Fflewddur.

"Finally, I turned to brewing my own potions," said Glew. "I wanted to be fierce! I wanted to be strong, to make all Mona tremble! Oh, it was long labor, I tell you. Alas, you see the results. And the end of all my hopes," the giant glumly continued. "Until you came along. You must help me escape from this frightful cavern. I can't stand the bats and the crawly things. It's too much, I tell you, too much! It's nasty and horrid and sticky and wet," he cried in loud despair. "I can't abide mold and mushrooms! Mold and mushrooms! I've had enough of them!" He set to weeping again and his pitiful moans shook the cavern.

"Dallben, my master, is the most powerful enchanter in Prydain," Taran said. "It may be that he can find a means to help you. But it is your help we need now. The sooner we are free, the sooner I shall return to him."

"Too long to wait," moaned Glew. "I'll be a mushroom myself by that time."

"Help us," Taran pleaded. "Help us and we shall try to help you."

Glew said nothing for a moment. His forehead wrinkled and his lips twitched nervously. "Very well, very well," he sighed, climbing to his feet. "Follow me. Oh—there's one thing you might do," he added. "If it would be no bother to you, it's such a little thing, if you really wouldn't mind. So at least I might have the satisfaction, however brief. A tiny favor. Would you call me—King Glew?"

"Great Belin," shouted Fflewddur, "I'll call you king, prince, or whatever you choose. Only show us a way out of here—Sire!"

Glew's spirits seemed to lift as he shambled toward the dim reaches of the cavern. The companions scrambled down the ledge and hastened to keep up with his huge strides. Glew, having spoken to no one since his confinement, never left off talking. He had, he explained, tried to brew new potions —this time to make himself smaller. In one of the chambers he had even set up a kind of workshop, where a bubbling pool of steaming hot water served to boil his concoctions. Glew's cleverness in devising makeshift pestles and mortars, cookpots and basins from painstakingly hollowed-out stones surprised Taran and filled him with a pitying admiration for the desperate giant. But his mind turned over and over on itself, seeking an understanding that escaped him like a will-o'-the-wisp each time he drew close to it. He was certain the answer lay in the ruined halls of Caer Colur, and certain the companions would find Eilonwy there.

Impatient to be gone, he ran forward as Glew halted at a chimney-like shaft of rock. Close to the ground the dark mouth of a tunnel opened.

"Farewell," sniffed Glew, pointing sorrowfully at the tunnel. "Go straight on. You shall find your way."

"You have my word," Taran said, while Gurgi, Fflewddur, and Prince Rhun crawled into the opening. "If it is in Dallben's power, he will help you."

Clutching the bauble, Taran bent and thrust his way past the jagged arch. Bats rose in a shrieking cloud. He heard Gurgi cry out in fear and raced ahead. Next moment, he collided with a wall of stone and fell back on his heels while the bauble slipped from his grasp and dropped among the pebbles on the uneven ground. With a shout Taran spun to see a massive rock pushed into the opening, and flung himself toward it.

Glew had sealed the passage.

CHAPTER XII

The Tomb

The bard, like Taran, had dashed headlong into the wall, and now struggled to his feet. Gurgi's yells rang above the screeching of the bats. Prince Rhun stumbled to Taran's side and threw his weight against the immovable rock. The bauble had rolled into a corner, but one glance, in the light of the glowing sphere, showed Taran there was no other way in or out of the chamber.

"Glew!" Taran called, pushing with all his strength at the blocked passage. "Let us out! What have you done!"

While Gurgi, jabbering furiously, beat his fists against the unyielding stone, Taran plunged against it once more. Beside him, he heard Prince Rhun gasping with his own efforts. Fflewddur shoved and heaved mightily, lost his footing, and sprawled to earth.

"Little worm!" the bard shouted at the top of his voice. "Liar! You've betrayed us!"

From the other side of the stone came Glew's muffled voice, "I'm very sorry. Forgive me. But what else am I to do?"

"Let us out!" Taran demanded again, still straining to move the rock. With a sob half of anger and half of despair, he dropped to earth and scrabbled desperately at the loose pebbles.

"Move aside heavy stone, evil, wicked little giant!" shouted Gurgi. "Take away lockings and blockings! Or rageful Gurgi will smack your great feeble head!"

"We would have done you a kindness," Taran cried. "And you repay us with treachery."

"I say, that's true enough," called Prince Rhun. "How do you expect anyone to help you if they're buried in here?"

Faint though it was, a sobbing sound drifted from beyond the blocked passageway. "Too long!" moaned the voice of Glew. "Too long! I can wait no more in this ghastly cave! Who knows whether Dallben would care about my fate? Very likely he wouldn't. It must be done now. Now!"

"Glew," Taran said, forcing himself to be as calm and patient as he could, for he was convinced the giant had taken leave of his senses, "there is nothing we alone can do for you or we would have done it before this."

"But there is! There is!" cried Glew. "You shall help with my potions. I'm sure I can brew another to bring me back to size. That's all I ask. Is that too much?"

"If you want us to help you cook up more of those dreadful messes you fed Llyan," called Fflewddur, "you're taking a curious way to win our friendship." The bard hesitated and his eyes widened in sudden dismay. "Great Belin," he murmured, "as he did with Llyan . . . !"

Even as the bard spoke, Taran's legs began to quake, for the same thought had occurred to him. "Fflewddur," he whispered, "he is indeed out of his wits. This cavern has driven him mad."

"Not a bit of it," replied the bard. "It makes excellent sense, in a nasty, horrible fashion. He has no one else to try his concoctions on!" He pressed to the stone and cupped his hands around his mouth. "You shan't do that, you wretched, sniveling worm!" he shouted. "We won't swallow your evil stews! Even if you starve us! And if you try to cram them down our throats, you'll learn that a Fflam can bite!"

"I promise," pleaded Glew, "you won't have to swallow a thing. I'll take all the risks myself. Terrible risks they are, too. Suppose I should turn into a puff of smoke and blow away? You never know, when you're dealing with such recipes. It could happen."

"I wish it would," muttered Fflewddur.

"No, no," Glew went on, "this won't hurt you a bit, you can be sure. It won't take more than a moment of your time. Half a moment! And I shall only need one of you. Only one! You can't say that's asking too much, you can't be so selfish . . ."

Glew's voice had risen to a frenzy and he had begun shouting and wailing so loudly and rapidly Taran could barely make out the words; but as he listened, Taran felt the blood drain from his heart, a chill held and shook him as Glew babbled on.

"Glew," he cried, despair welling up in him, "what do you mean to do with us?"

"Please, please try to understand," returned Glew's voice. "It's my only chance. I'm sure it will work. I've thought it over carefully ever since I've been in this awful hole. I know I can brew the right potion; I have all I need. Except one thing. One tiny little ingredient. It won't hurt you a bit; you won't feel a thing, I swear it to you."

Taran gasped in horror. "You mean to kill one of us!"

There was a long silence. Finally Glew's voice reached the companions again; it sounded as though Glew's feelings had been hurt. "You make it sound so—so raw!"

"Great Belin," shouted Fflewddur, "let me get my hands on your scrawny neck and I'll make *you* sound raw!"

There was another silence. "Please," said Glew faintly, "try to look at it from my side."

"Gladly," said Fflewddur. "Just push away that rock."

"Don't think it's easy for me," Glew went on. "I'm fond of all of you, especially the little fuzzy one; and I feel dreadful about the whole thing. But there's no chance anyone else will stop down here. You do understand that, don't you? You aren't angry? I'd never forgive myself if you were.

"Even now," he added plaintively, "I don't know how I'll ever bring myself to pick out one of you. No, no, I can't. I haven't the heart. Don't ask me to put myself through that torment. No, you shall decide among you. That will be best all around.

"Believe me," Glew continued, "it will be worse for me than for you. But I'll shut my eyes, so I won't see which one of you it is. Then, after it's over, we'll try to forget about it. We'll be the best of good friends—those of you remaining, that is. I'll lead you out of here, I promise. We'll find Llyan—oh, it will be good to see her again—and all will be well.

"Don't go away," said Glew. "I'll get a few things ready. I won't keep you waiting."

"Glew, listen to me!" called Taran. "This is an evil deed you plan. Set us free!"

No answer came. The rock did not move.

"Dig, friends!" cried Fflewddur, drawing his sword. "Dig for your lives!"

Taran and Gurgi unsheathed their blades and, side by side, attacked the ground beneath the ponderous stone. With all their strength they thrust into the rocky, unyielding earth. Their swordpoints rang on the pebbles, but try as they would they could barely scrape away more than a shallow hole. Prince Rhun sought to force his sword under the rock but succeeded only in snapping the point off the blade.

Taran picked up the bauble. Bending to hands and knees, he scanned every portion of this prison, hoping to find some crack or tiny opening the companions could enlarge. The walls rose sheer and unbroken.

"He has trapped us well," said Taran, sinking

to the ground. "There is but one way out. The way Glew offers us."

"As I consider it," said Rhun, "he asked for only one of us. That would leave three to keep searching for the Princess."

Taran was thoughtful for a moment. "For the first time," he said bitterly, "I believed I had guessed where Magg meant to bring Eilonwy. To Caer Colur. It is the strongest clue we have gained. Now it is useless to us."

"Useless?" said Rhun. "Not at all. We need only do as Glew suggests, and the others can be on their way."

"Do you expect that feeble worm to keep his word?" Fflewddur asked angrily. "I would trust him every bit as much as I would trust Magg."

"Nevertheless," said Rhun, "we can't be sure until we try."

The companions fell silent at the Prince of Mona's words. Gurgi, who had crouched on the earth and wrapped his woolly arms around his knees, stared wretchedly at Taran. "Gurgi will go," the creature whispered faintly, though he trembled so much he could hardly speak. "Yes, yes, he will give his poor tender head for broilings and boilings."

"Valiant Gurgi," murmured Taran. "Indeed I know you would give up your poor tender head." He patted the frightened Gurgi. "But there is no question of that. We must stand together. If Glew wants a life, he shall pay dearly for it."

Fflewddur once more began digging and chipping at the rock. "I agree with you entirely," he said. "We must stand as one—to the extent that we have any choice at all. As soon as the little fellow comes back—oh, drat and blast—I don't know why I keep thinking of him as a little fellow, except that he impresses me that way no matter what his size. He'll surely seize one of us. He hasn't the honor of a flea or the heart of a gnat, and he's desperate. If we fight him, there's a good chance all of us shall be slain."

"You cannot mean we should take Glew's bargain," said Taran.

"Certainly not," replied Fflewddur, "I shall stand sword in hand and smite the little fellow about the knees since I can't reach his head. I only mean to point out the risks. As far as his ridiculous idea of having us choose among ourselves is concerned, I don't think it even worth a thought."

"I do," said Prince Rhun.

Taran turned in surprise to Rhun, not fully understanding his words. The Prince of Mona grinned at him almost shyly.

"It's the only thing that will satisfy Glew," said Rhun, "and for that I think it's a very cheap bargain."

"No life can be so cheaply held," Taran began.

"I'm afraid you're wrong," answered Rhun. He smiled and shook his head. "I've thought a great deal about this since we've been in the cavern, and there's no sense not facing facts. I—I don't see that I've been any help whatever. On the contrary, I've brought nothing but ill luck. Not that I meant to, but it seems that's the way of it with me. So, if any one of us can be dispensed with, why, I should have to say that person is——myself.

"It's true," Rhun quickly went on, disregarding Taran's cry of protest. "I'm delighted to be of some use for once, especially if it will help Eilonwy. I assure you I won't mind in the slightest. As Glew says, it will only take a moment.

"There's not one of you who wouldn't give up his life for a companion," Rhun added. "Fflewddur Fflam offered his life for ours in Llyan's lair. Even now poor Gurgi is willing to offer his." He raised his head. "A bard, a humble creature of the forest, an Assistant Pig-Keeper." Rhun's eyes met Taran's and in a low voice he said, "Can a Prince do less? I doubt I should ever really be able to measure up to being a true Prince. Except in this."

Taran looked at Rhun for a long moment. "You speak of measure," he said. "I had measured you as no more than a feckless princeling. I was wrong. You are a truer Prince and better man than ever I believed. But this sacrifice is not yours to make. You know my oath to your father."

Prince Rhun grinned again. "Indeed, a heavy oath," he said. "Very well, I shall lift it from you. I say," he added, "it's astonishing, but I wonder what became of all the bats?"

CHAPTER XIII

The Ladder

hy—they're gone!" Taran quickly flashed the golden light about the chamber. "Every one of them!"

"Yes, yes," Gurgi cried. "No more shriekings and squeakings!"

"I can't say I'm unhappy about it," added the bard. "I get along well enough with mice, and I've always been fond of birds, but when you put the two together I'd just as soon avoid them."

"The bats may prove our best friends and surest guides," Taran said. "Rhun has struck on something. The bats have found a way out. If we can only discover it, we can follow them."

"Quite so," answered the bard, making a wry face. "First thing would be to turn into bats ourselves. Then, I daresay, we should have no difficulties."

Taran strode hurriedly from one end of the chamber to the other. He played the bauble's light over the walls, sending the beams upward to the sloping ceiling of rock, scanning each crevice and outcropping, but saw only a few shallow niches from which some ancient stone had fallen.

Again and again he swept the golden light around the cave. A faint, shadowy line seemed traced amid the stones high above him. He stepped back and studied it carefully. The shadow deepened, and Taran realized it marked a narrow ledge, a flaw in the rock. "There it is!" he called, holding the bauble as steadily as his trembling hands allowed. "There—you can barely make it out, the wall curves and hides it. But see where the rock seems to dip and break . . ."

"Amazing!" cried Rhun. "Astonishing! It's a passage, rightly enough. The bats have gone through it. Do you think we can?"

Setting the golden sphere on the ground, Taran strode to the rock face and sought to raise himself by grasping the slight ripples of stone; but the wall was too sheer, his hands slipped, clutched vainly for support, and he fell back before he had been able to climb his own height. Gurgi, too, attempted to scale the smooth surface. For all his agility, he did little better than Taran and he sank down, puffing and moaning.

"Just as I said," glumly remarked Fflewddur. "All we need is a few pairs of wings."

Taran had not ceased to stare at the high passageway taunting him with the promise of freedom beyond his reach. "We cannot climb the wall," he said, frowning, "but there may still be hope." His eyes turned from the distant ledge to the companions, then back again. "A rope would not help us, even if we had one. There is no means of securing it. But a ladder . . ."

"Exactly what we need," said Fflewddur. "But unless you're prepared to build one on the spot, we shouldn't waste our time grieving over something we don't have."

"We can build a ladder," Taran said quietly. "Yes. I should have seen it at once."

"What, what?" cried the bard. "A Fflam is clever, but you're going far beyond me."

"We can do it," replied Taran, "and need seek no further. We ourselves are the ladder."

"Great Belin!" shouted Fflewddur, clapping his hands. "Of course! Yes, we shall climb on each other's shoulders." He ran to the wall and measured it with a glance. "Still too high," he said, shaking his head. "Even the topmost man would reach it with little to spare."

"But he would reach it, nevertheless," insisted Taran. "It is our only escape."

"*His* only escape," corrected the bard. "Whoever climbs out will shorten our ladder by that much. Our choice is hardly better than what Glew gave us," he added. "Only one of us can save himself."

Taran nodded. "It may be that he can drop a vine down to the others," he said. "In that way . . ." He stopped.

Glew's voice filtered into the chamber. "Is all well in there?" called the giant. "It's going splendidly out here. I've made everything ready. I hope you're not too upset. Would one of you mind stepping forward? Don't tell me which; I don't want to know. I'm as sorry as you are."

Taran turned quickly to the Prince of Mona. "I know their hearts and I speak for my companions. Our choice is taken. It is too late to hope to save us. Try to make your way to Caer Colur. Should Kaw find you, he will guide you there."

"I don't intend leaving anyone behind," replied Rhun. "If this is your choice, it is not mine. I shall not . . ."

"Prince Rhun," Taran said firmly. "Did you not put yourself under my orders?" The stone had begun to grate in the passageway and Taran could hear Glew's frantic snuffling. "This, too, you must take," he said, pressing the bauble into Rhun's reluctant hand. "It is rightfully Eilonwy's and it is you who shall give it back to her." He turned his eyes away. "May it shine brightly on your wedding day."

Gurgi had clambered to the shoulders of the bard, who braced himself against the wall. Rhun still hesitated. Taran seized him by the collar of his jacket and dragged him forward.

Taran climbed to Fflewddur's back, then to Gurgi's. The human ladder swayed dangerously. Under the weight of the companions, the bard cried for Rhun to hurry. Taran felt Rhun's hands grasp at him, then slip. From below came Gurgi's labored breathing. Taran clutched Rhun's belt and heaved upward, as one knee then the other was thrust upon his shoulders.

"The passage is too far," gasped Rhun.

"Stand up," Taran cried. "Steady. You're nearly there."

With a last effort, he forced himself to rise as high as he could. Rhun scrabbled at the ledge. Suddenly Taran's burden was lifted.

"Farewell, Prince of Mona," he called, as Rhun swung himself to the narrow outcropping and plunged into the passage.

Fflewddur cried a warning and Taran felt himself falling. Dazed and breathless on the stones, he tried to regain his feet. It was utterly dark. He staggered against the bard who pulled him from what Taran realized was the entry to the chamber. A rush of chill air told Taran that Glew had pushed the rock aside, and he sensed, rather than saw, a darker shadow thrust into the opening. Taran unsheathed his blade and swung it wildly. It struck something solid.

"Ah! Ow!" cried Glew. "You mustn't do that!"

The arm pulled back suddenly. Taran heard Fflewddur draw his blade. Gurgi had scuttled to Taran's side and was throwing stones as fast as he could pick them up.

"We must stand against him now!" Taran cried. "We shall see whether he's as great a coward as he is a liar. Hurry! Give him no chance to shut us in again!"

Swords raised, the companions flung themselves out of the chamber. Somewhere, Taran knew, Glew towered above them; but in the blackness he dared not strike with his weapon, fearful of harming Gurgi or Fflewddur stumbling along next to him.

"You're spoiling it all!" wailed Glew. "I shall have to catch one of you myself. Why are you making me do this? I thought you understood! I thought you wanted to help me!"

Wind whistled over Taran's head as Glew snatched at him. He threw himself down among the sharp rocks. To one side he heard Fflewddur shout, "Great Belin, the little monster can see better in the dark than we can!" Until now the companions had clung together, but Taran's sudden movement had torn him away from the others. He groped to rejoin them and, at the same time, to escape Glew's frantic lunges.

He tumbled against a pile of stones that gave way with a clatter, and went sliding into a stream of noisome liquid.

Glew wailed in resounding despair. "Now you've done it! You've upset my potions! Stop it, stop it, you're making a mess of everything!"

What must have been Glew's foot came stamping down nearly on top of him, as Taran lashed out with his sword. The blade rebounded in his hand, but Glew yelled horribly. Above Taran an almost invisible shadow seemed to be hopping on one leg. The bard was right, Taran thought in terror; the greatest risk from Glew lay in being trampled. The ground shook under the giant's feet and Taran leaped blindly from the sound.

Next thing he knew, he fell with a splash into one of the pools dotting the cavern. He thrashed wildly and flung out his arms, seeking a handhold on the rocky edge. The water glittered with a cold, pale light. As Taran scrambled out, bright, luminous droplets clung to his drenched garments, his face, hands, and hair. Escape for him was hopeless now; the glow would betray him wherever he sought refuge.

"Run!" Taran shouted to the companions. "Let Glew follow me!"

In one stride the giant was at the pool. By the light of his own dripping body, Taran could make out the huge shape. He thrust forward with his blade. The eager hand of Glew brushed it aside.

"Please, please, I beg you," cried Glew, "don't make things worse than they are! Even now I shall have to boil my potion again. Have you no consideration? No thought for anyone else?"

The giant reached to seize him. Taran raised his sword high above his head in a last futile gesture of defense.

Golden rays burst around him, brilliant as noonday.

With a scream of pain, Glew clapped his hands to his eyes. "The light!" he shrieked. "Stop the light!"

Screaming and roaring, the giant covered his head with his arms. His earsplitting bellows rang through the cave. The stone icicles trembled and crashed to earth; the crystals split and showered Taran with fragments. Suddenly Glew was no longer standing, but stretched full length, half covered by the shards, lying motionless where a falling crystal

had glanced off his head. Taran, still dazzled, leaped
to his feet.

At the entrance to the chamber stood Prince
Rhun, the bauble blazing in his hand.

CHAPTER XIV

The Empty Book

ullo, hullo!" called Rhun, hastening to the companions. "I've never been so surprised in my life. I didn't mean to disobey orders, but after I'd crawled out the passage, I—I just couldn't leave you there to be cooked up; I simply couldn't do it. I kept thinking to myself that none of you would have gone running off . . ." He hesitated and looked anxiously at Taran. "You aren't angry are you?"

"You saved our lives," replied Taran. He clasped Rhun's hand. "I only reproach you for risking your own."

"Joy and happiness!" cried Gurgi. "Poor tender head is spared from stampings and trampings! And kind master is safe from brewings and stewings!"

"But the most amazing thing was the bauble," Prince Rhun went on, beaming proudly. "The light didn't go out, even after I'd got hold of it. Astonishing!" He stared curiously at the golden sphere, whose rays had already begun to dim, and handed it back to Taran. "I don't know what happened. It suddenly started getting bright and brighter, all of itself. Unbelievable!"

"It's the one thing that stopped him," said Fflewddur. Hands on hips, the bard was looking down at the prostrate form of Glew. "He'd been here so long he couldn't stand the brightness, the repulsive little grub. There, I'm calling him little again," he added. "But I still say for a giant he's remarkably small-natured." He knelt and peered at Glew's face. "He's had a good crack on the head, but he's still alive." Fflewddur put a hand to his sword. "We might be wise to—ah—make sure he doesn't wake up."

"Leave him," said Taran, staying Fflewddur's arm. "I know he tried to do us ill, but I still pity the wretched creature and mean to ask Dallben if he can help him."

"Very well," said Fflewddur with some reluctance. "He wouldn't have done as much for us. But, a Fflam is merciful! Quick, now, let's be off."

"How did you climb down?" Taran asked Rhun. "Did you find vines long enough to reach us?"

Prince Rhun's jaw dropped and he blinked with alarm. "I—I'm afraid I've done it again," he murmured. "I didn't climb. I jumped. I somehow never thought of getting out again. Surprising, it simply never occurred to me. I'm sorry, I've put us right back where we were."

"Not quite," replied Taran to the despondent Prince. "We can hoist you up as we did before, and this time you can lower something for the rest of us. But we must make haste."

"There's no need for us to stand on each other's heads," Fflewddur suddenly cried. "I see an easier way. Look there!" He pointed upward to where a large crack yawned in the cavern wall. A shaft of sunlight fell over the stones and fresh air whistled through the crevice. "We can thank Glew for that. With all his roaring and screaming he's shaken the rocks loose. We shall be out in no time! Bless the repulsive little monster! He said he wanted to make Mona tremble," he added, "and, Great Belin, so he did—after a fashion!"

The companions hurried to the wall of the cave and began picking their way through the rubble of broken stones. Prince Rhun, however, halted abruptly and began fumbling with his jacket.

"I say, that's surprising," he cried. "I know I put it there." With an anxious frown he began searching his garments once again.

"Hurry," Taran called. "We dare not be here when Glew comes to his senses. What are you looking for?"

"My book," answered Rhun. "Where can it be? It must have fallen out while I was crawling through that hole. Or perhaps . . ."

"Leave it!" Taran urged. "It is worthless. You've risked your life once. Don't risk it again for a book of empty pages!"

"It was a handsome keepsake," said Rhun, "and would be useful. It can't be far. Go ahead, I'll join you. I shan't be a moment." He turned and trotted back toward the tunnel.

"Rhun!" Taran shouted, racing after him. The

Prince of Mona disappeared into the chamber. Taran found him on hands and knees groping over the rough floor.

"Splendid!" cried Rhun, glancing over his shoulder. "A little light is what I needed. Now, surely, it's bound to be here. Let me see, first, where I was climbing up. If it dropped out then, by all rights it should be close to the wall."

Taran was determined, if need be, to lay hold of the Prince and drag him bodily from the cell which had so nearly become a tomb. He strode forward just as Rhun gave a cry of triumph.

"And there it is!" shouted the Prince, He picked up the book and carefully examined it. "I hope it isn't damaged," he remarked. "All that scrambling about might have torn the pages. No, it seems . . ." He stopped and shook his head in dismay. "I say, that is a shame! It's ruined. All covered with scratchings and markings. Whatever could have happened?"

He put the leather-bound volume into Taran's hand. "Look," he said. "What a pity. Every page is marred. It's really useless now."

Taran was about to cast the book aside and carry out his first intention of collaring the Prince, but his eyes widened at the sight of the pages. "Rhun," he whispered, "these are more than scratchings. It is carefully written. I had thought the pages empty."

"So had I," said Rhun. "What could . . ."

Fflewddur called out, urging them to hasten.

Taran and Prince Rhun left the chamber. Gurgi had already reached the opening in the cavern ceiling and was beckoning to them.

"The book we found in Glew's hut," Taran began.

"Don't worry about Glew's property, worry about Glew," said Fflewddur. "He's beginning to stir. Move along or we'll still end up in one of his potions."

The sun had just risen, but it was bright and warming after the dank cavern. The companions gratefully breathed the fresh springtime air. Gurgi shouted joyfully and raced on ahead. He soon returned with good tidings: the river lay not too far away. The companions set out for it with all speed.

As they strode along Taran held up the volume to Fflewddur. "There is deep mystery in this. I cannot read the writing; the script is ancient. But how it came there . . ."

"After what we've been through," replied the bard, glancing at the pages, "I can understand your wanting to jest. But this is hardly the moment for it."

"Jest? I do not jest!" Taran started as he pointed at the volume again. The pages were empty as they had always been. "The writing," he stammered. "It's gone!"

"My friend," said the bard gently, "your eyes have played you false. At the river we'll put cool cloths on your head and you'll feel much better. It's quite understandable, considering the darkness, the shock of nearly being boiled . . ."

"I know what I have seen," Taran protested. "Even in the cavern, even in the dim light of the bauble . . ."

"It's true," put in Rhun, who had been following their talk. "I saw it myself. There's no mistake. The bauble was shining straight on the pages."

"The bauble!" Taran cried. "Wait! Can it be?" Hurriedly he drew out the sphere, while the companions halted and watched him silently. As the light blossomed in his hand, Taran held it so that its rays bathed the pages in a golden glow.

The writing sprang into sight, sharp and clear.

"Astonishing!" cried Rhun. "The most amazing thing I've seen in my life!"

Taran crouched on the turf, held the bauble close to the book, and with trembling fingers turned leaf after leaf. The curious tracing crowded every page. The bard gave a long, low whistle.

"What does this mean, Fflewddur?" Taran asked. He raised his head and looked with concern at the bard.

The bard's face had paled. "What it means, in my opinion," said Fflewddur, "is that we should get rid of the book instantly. Drop it in the river. I regret to say I can't read it. I could never manage to learn all these secret scripts and ancient letters. But I recognize enchantment when I see it." He shuddered and turned away. "I'd rather not even look at it, if you don't mind. Not that it frightens me. Yes, it makes me feel acutely uneasy; and you know my views on meddling."

"If Glew spoke the truth, it comes from a place

of enchantments," Taran said. "But what can it tell us? I shall not destroy it," he added, returning the book to his jacket. "I can't explain; I feel as though I'd touched a secret. It's strange, like a moth that brushes your hand and flutters away again."

"Ahem," said Fflewddur, casting a nervous glance at Taran. "If you insist on carrying the thing with you, would you oblige me—nothing personal, you understand—but I would appreciate it if you'd stay a few paces away."

Midday was long past when the companions reached the riverbank, but they rejoiced at their good fortune. The remains of the raft were still there. They set to work hastily to repair it. Prince Rhun, in better spirits than ever, labored unstintingly. For a time Taran had forgotten the Prince of Mona was to be Eilonwy's betrothed. Now the sad thought returned to him as he helped Rhun knot new vines around the raft.

"You should be proud of yourself," Taran said quietly. "Did you seek to prove yourself a true Prince? You have done so, Rhun Son of Rhuddlum."

"Why, perhaps that's so," replied Rhun, as though the idea had never occurred to him. "But it's a curious thing. It doesn't seem one bit as important as it did. Astonishing, but true!"

The sun had begun to dip by the time the raft was ready. Taran, who had grown more and more restless as the day waned, urged the companions to press on rather than wait the night on shore, and they clambered aboard.

Twilight soon fell over the valley, and the Alaw ran in swift silver ripples under the rising moon. The shore lay silent, flanked by brooding hills. In the middle of the raft Gurgi curled up like a muddy ball of leaves; beside him, the Prince of Mona slept and snored peacefully, a smile of contentment on his round face. Taking the first watch, Taran and Fflewddur guided the awkward craft as it rapidly floated seaward.

They spoke little. Fflewddur had not entirely lost his disquiet over the strange book. Taran's thoughts were for the morrow, which he hoped would bring the companions closer to the end of their search. Once again, fear and doubt made him wonder if he had chosen wisely. Even if Eilonwy had been taken to Caer Colur, he had no cause to believe Magg—or Achren—still held her there. So little was known for certain. The book and its meaning, even the nature of Eilonwy's bauble, were more riddles added to so many others.

"Why?" he murmured. "Why is the writing clear only when the bauble shines on it? And why did it light for Rhun, when it had never done so before? Why did it light for me, for that matter?"

"As a bard," answered Fflewddur, "I know a great deal about these enchanted devices, and I can tell you . . ." At the narrow end of the harp, a string tinkled as it snapped in two. "Ah, yes," said Fflewddur, "the fact is: I know very little about them. Eilonwy, of course, has the gift of making it light when she pleases. She's half an enchantress, you know, and the bauble does belong to her. For someone else, I wonder—and I'm only guessing, mind you—I wonder if it might have to do with—how shall I put it—not even thinking about it. Or about yourself.

"What I mean," Fflewddur went on, "in the cavern, when I tried to make it light, I was saying to myself: If *I* can do this, if *I* can find the way for us . . ."

"Perhaps," Taran said quietly, watching the moon-white riverbank slip past them, "perhaps you have the truth of it. At first I felt as you did. Then I remember thinking of Eilonwy, only of her; and the bauble showed its light. Prince Rhun was ready to lay down his life; his thoughts were for our safety, not at all for his own. And because he offered the greatest sacrifice, the bauble glowed brightest for him. Can that be its secret? To think more for others than ourselves?"

"That would seem to be one of its secrets, at least," replied Fflewddur. "Once you've discovered that, you've discovered a great secret indeed—with or without the bauble."

The hills had flattened and given way to low fields of sedge. A scent of brine and brackish water reached Taran's nostrils. Ahead, the river widened, flowing into a bay, and beyond that to an even greater expanse of water. To his right, on the far side of towering rocks, Taran heard the rush of surf. Reluctantly he decided they dared go no farther until dawn. While Fflewddur roused Gurgi and Prince Rhun, Taran poled the raft to shore.

The companions settled themselves amid a tall clump of reeds and Gurgi opened his wallet of food. Taran, still restless, walked to a hillock and peered toward the sea.

"Keep to the shadows," said the voice of Gwydion. "Achren's eyes are sharp."

CHAPTER XV

The Island

The Prince of Don rose like a shadow from the sedge. Though he had discarded his head-cloth and tools, he still wore the shabby raiment of his disguise. Perched on Gwydion's shoulder, Kaw blinked and ruffled his feathers, indignant at being awakened; seeing Taran, however, he bobbed his head and began croaking with excitement.

Taran, startled, cried out. Prince Rhun, waving his sword with great vigor and making as fierce a face as he could, hastened to join Taran.

"Why, it looks like the shoemaker!" Rhun called, lowering his weapon as he caught sight of the tall figure. "Is it, indeed? Whatever have you done with those sandals you promised?"

"Alas, Prince Rhun," Gwydion replied, "your sandals must wait on other matters."

"This is no shoemaker but Gwydion Prince of Don," Taran hurriedly whispered.

Gurgi and Fflewddur had now run up. The bard's jaw dropped.

"Great Belin!" stammered Fflewddur. "To

think we shared a stable at Dinas Rhydnant! Lord Gwydion, had you only made yourself known to me . . ."

"Forgive me for deceiving you," answered Gwydion. "I dared not do otherwise. Silence then was my best shield."

"I would have sought you at Dinas Rhydnant," Taran said, "but Magg gave us no time. He has stolen away Eilonwy. We have been told of a place called Caer Colur where he might have taken her and have been trying to make our way there."

"Thanks to Kaw, I know a little of what has befallen you," Gwydion said. "He told me you had chosen to follow the river. He lost you when Llyan pursued him, but found me here.

"Achren, too, sought Caer Colur," Gwydion went on quickly. "When I learned this, I strove to follow her ship. One of the fisherfolk sailed with me to the northern coast. Your island people are bold," he added, glancing at Rhun. "Remember them with honor when you shall be King of Mona. The fisherman would have brought me to Caer Colur itself. This favor I could not accept, for I dared not reveal my mission to him. Yet before he returned to Mona Haven, he willingly gave me the small boat he carried aboard, and would take no reward for his risk or his generosity."

"Have you already gone to Caer Colur?" Taran asked. "Was there any trace of Eilonwy?"

Gwydion nodded. "Yes. But I have failed to save the Princess," he said heavily. "She is Achren's prisoner. Magg moved more swiftly than any of us."

"The spider!" cried the bard with such heat that Kaw started up in alarm. "The sneering, sneaking spider! I beg you, let me deal with him. He and I have a long score to settle and it grows longer every moment!" He raised his sword. "I shan't need this! When I find him, I'll squash him with my bare hands!"

"Hold hold," ordered Gwydion. "Spider he may be, but his sting is all the more deadly. His vanity and ambition have made him Achren's willing creature. He shall be dealt with, and so shall Achren. Our concern now is for Eilonwy."

"Can we not free her?" Taran asked. "How closely is she guarded?"

"Last night I rowed to the island," Gwydion said. "In the little time I remained there, I could not discover where the Princess is held. Though I saw that Achren has but a paltry company of warriors—hirelings and outlaws who have cast their lot with her. None of Arawn's deathless Cauldron-Born is among them." He smiled bitterly. "Without the protection of the Lord of Annuvin, haughty Achren commands only lackeys."

"Then we can attack them now," Taran cried, his hand on his sword. "We are enough to overcome them."

"This task calls for strength of a different nature, and swords are not all we shall have to fear," Gwydion replied. "There is much I have not told you of this matter, and much that I myself did not know. Even now the riddle is not fully answered. But I have learned that Achren's plans are deeper than I had imagined, and Eilonwy's plight graver. She must be taken from Caer Colur before it is too late."

Gwydion drew his cloak around him and stepped toward the riverbank. Taran caught his arm. "Let us go with you," he urged. "We shall stand with you should you need us and guard Eilonwy's escape."

The tall warrior paused and glanced at the waiting companions. He turned his green-flecked eyes on Taran and studied him closely. "I do not doubt the courage of any one of you. But Caer Colur holds greater peril than you know."

"Eilonwy is dear to me, to all of us," Taran said.

Gwydion was silent a moment, his weathered face grim and withdrawn. Then he nodded. "It shall be as you wish. Follow me."

The Prince of Don led the companions from the marshy fields to a narrow shoulder of beach. From there, they passed along the edge of the sea to a sheltered cove, where a small boat bobbed at the end of a mooring line. Gwydion beckoned the companions to step aboard, took the oars, and with swift noiseless strokes guided the little craft seaward.

As the glittering black water rolled beneath him, Taran crouched in the bow of the boat and strained his eyes for a sign of Caer Colur. Prince Rhun and the companions huddled at the stern, while Gwydion bent his powerful shoulders to the oars. The stars had begun to fade and banks of sea mist drifted in chill clouds.

"Our task must be finished quickly and before daylight," said Gwydion. "Most of Achren's warriors have been set to guard the landward entry. We shall land on the far side of the castle, hard by the outer wall. In darkness we may escape their eyes."

"Glew told us Caer Colur had broken from the mainland," said Taran, "but I had not imagined it to be this far at sea."

Gwydion frowned. "Glew? Kaw said nothing to me of Glew."

"It was then that Kaw left us," Taran explained. "Small wonder he could not find us again, for we were deep underground." He told Gwydion of finding Eilonwy's bauble, the treachery of Glew, and the strange book. Gwydion, who had been listening intently, shipped the oars and let the boat drift.

"Alas that you did not speak of this sooner. I would have found better means of safeguarding it," he said, as Taran handed him the golden sphere which began to glow brightly. Gwydion spread his cloak and shielded the light. Quickly he took the book from Taran's hands, opened it, and brought the bauble closer to the empty pages. The ancient writing sprang into sight. Gwydion's face was tense and pale.

"To read this is beyond my power," Gwydion said, "but I recognize it for what it is: the greatest treasure of the House of Llyr."

"A treasure of Llyr?" Taran whispered, "What is its nature? Does it belong to Eilonwy?"

Gwydion nodded. "She is the last Princess of Llyr, and it is hers by blood-right. But there is more you must understand. For generations the daughters of the House of Llyr were among the most skillful enchantresses in Prydain, using their powers with wisdom and kindliness. In their fastness at Caer Colur were stored all their treasures, magical devices and charmed implements whose nature even I do not know.

"The chronicles of the House of Llyr give only veiled hints as to how these mysteries were guarded. The lore tells of an enchantment known only as the Golden Pelydryn, handed down from mother to daughter, and of a book holding all the secrets of those magical devices and many potent spells.

"But Caer Colur was abandoned and fell into ruins after Angharad Daughter of Regat fled the castle to marry against her mother's wishes. The book of spells, which she carried away with her, was believed lost. Of the Golden Pelydryn, nothing was known." Gwydion looked down at the bauble. "The Golden Pelydryn was not lost. What better way to hide it than to put it as a shining toy in the hands of a child?

"Eilonwy believed she had been sent to live with Achren and study to be an enchantress," Gwydion went on. "It is not true. Achren stole Eilonwy and brought her as a child to Spiral Castle."

"Did Achren fail to recognize the Golden Pelydryn?" Taran asked. "If she knew its nature, why did she leave it in Eilonwy's possession?"

"Achren dared not do otherwise," answered Gwydion. "Yes, she knew Eilonwy's heritage. She recognized the Pelydryn, but also knew it would lose its power if taken forcibly from its rightful owner. Then, too, the book of spells had vanished. Achren could attempt nothing until it was found again."

"And without even realizing it," Taran said, "Glew was the one who gained the book of spells. Poor foolish creature who thought himself cheated!"

"So he was," replied Gwydion. "He could not have seen the hidden writing without the light of the Golden Pelydryn. Even then, it would have availed him nothing. The spells obey only a daughter of the House of Llyr. Eilonwy alone has the inborn skill to read them—though not before she herself has reached the threshold of womanhood. She stands there now, and the spells of Caer Colur are within her grasp. For that reason has Achren sought her so desperately."

"Eilonwy is safe, then," Taran cried. "If she alone can awaken the spells, Achren dares not harm her. Nor does Achren dare harm us, since the Pelydryn and the book of enchantments are in our hands."

"It may be," Gwydion answered grimly, "that Eilonwy is in greater danger than before."

Carefully Gwydion placed the book and golden sphere in his jacket and redoubled his efforts at the oars. Taran, clinging to the side of the boat, saw a high, dark mound loom ahead. Gwydion swung the craft farther seaward and now rowed steadily in a wide half-circle. The sea swell lifted the little vessel and drove it with ever-growing speed. The crash of waves rang in Taran's ears. Gwydion bent his strength to one oar, then the other, and Gurgi whimpered plaintively as the boat was flung forward into a narrow, foam-filled channel.

The pinnacles of Caer Colur rose black against a dark sky. Mist rolled around the columns of stone which had been, Taran guessed, proud and lofty towers, but were now crumbled and jutting ruins thrusting upward like the shards of broken swords. As they came closer, he saw the heavy, iron-bound portals, reminders of a day when Caer Colur had been a fortress rooted on the mainland. The gates faced the sea, but, since the castle had sunk lower, they stood half-submerged in the restless water. Waves churned and beat against them, as though to take the ruins by storm and wreak their last destruction.

Near the massive portals wind and water had gouged a cave-like hollow, and here Gwydion moored the boat and gestured for the companions to disembark. As they clambered to the rocks Taran heard a tormented groaning and creaking from the gates, as though they had gained their own voice and cried out against the onslaught of the waves. Gwydion climbed upward. Finding a handhold among the sharp stones, Rhun painfully toiled after him, with Taran and Gurgi following to catch the Prince of Mona should he fall. Fflewddur struggled along silently.

Kaw had already flown to the walls, and Taran envied the crow his wings as he saw the sheer facing of stone and the broken parapets brooding high above. Gwydion led them along the base of the wall toward the heavy lintels of the gates. The bastion was cleft as though by a sword stroke, and loose rubble had fallen into the breach. The Prince of Don signaled them to halt.

"Remain here," he ordered in a low voice. "I shall go first and learn where Achren's guards are posted." Noiselessly he vanished into the cleft. The companions crouched among the rocks not daring to speak.

Taran rested his head on his arms. His thoughts turned again and again to Eilonwy and to the words of Gwydion; he could barely bring himself to believe the slender, laughing girl could command powers perhaps as strong as those of Achren. Soon, soon, he told himself, Eilonwy would be free. But as his impatience grew, so did his fear, and he looked up anxiously, straining eyes and ears for a sign of Gwydion.

He was tempted then to follow the Prince of Don, but in another moment Gwydion appeared from the shadows. "Achren pays for a poor vigil," Gwydion said with a hard smile. "One sentinel watches landward, another leans drowsing on his sword. The others sleep."

The companions pressed through the cleft. The task now was to discover Eilonwy's prison, and Taran's heart sank. Within the walls the ruins of Caer Colur stretched like a great skeleton. Its tumble of once regal halls and towers lay before the companions, and Taran glanced with dismay at Gwydion. The tall warrior motioned for the companions to draw their swords and indicated where each of them was to search.

Fflewddur was about to move toward the out-lying buildings when Taran nearly cried aloud. Kaw fluttered from one of the towers and swooped down to perch on Taran's upraised arm. The crow beat his wings, flew aloft once more, and circled the pinnacle.

"He's found her!" Taran whispered. "Our search is over!"

"It has only now begun," warned Gwydion. "One of us shall climb up and see if it is possible to free her. The others shall take positions farther along the wall to guard against surprise by Achren's war-riors."

"I shall," Taran began, then hesitated and turned to Prince Rhun. He bowed his head. "She will be your betrothed. It was your wish that you . . ."

"That I should prove my valor to the Princess? Yes," Rhun said slowly. "But it is my wish no longer. I'm quite content proving it to myself. And I rather guess you might really be the one Eilonwy would prefer to see first."

Taran glanced at Gwydion, who nodded and directed the others to move to the landward side of the castle. As Rhun went to join Gurgi and Fflewddur, Gwydion knelt and drew the book and golden sphere from his jacket.

"If aught should go amiss, these must not fall into Achren's hands," he said, setting the objects care-fully beneath the loose stones. Deftly he replaced the rubble and smoothed the earth around it. "This must serve to guard them until we return."

Kaw had flown back to Taran. Gwydion rose

and from his belt took a coil of slender rope, made a loop on the end and held it out to Kaw, murmuring softly to the crow. The bird snatched the line with his beak and flapped silently to the jagged pinnacle, hovered above a jutting stone, then dropped the loop securely over it.

Gwydion turned to Taran. "I know what is in your heart," he said gently. "Climb up, Assistant Pig-Keeper. I leave this task to you."

Taran raced to the bottom of the tower. The rope pulled taut under his weight and the mist swirled about him, as he sought a foothold in the rough wall. He tightened his grip on the cord and drew himself upward. A sharp gust of sea wind buffeted him. For an instant he swung free of the tower. Below, the waves dashed against the rocks. He dared not look down, but desperately strove to halt the dizzying motion. His foot struck stone again. Bending all his strength to the rope, he climbed higher.

A casement opened just above him and Taran hoisted himself to the ledge. Within the small chamber a rush light burned fitfully. His heart leaped. Eilonwy was there.

The Princess lay motionless on a low couch. She still wore the robe Teleria had given her, though now it was torn and mud-spattered. The red-gold hair tumbled about her shoulders and her face was pale and drawn.

Taran hurriedly swung himself over the ledge, dropped to the flagstones, and hastened to Eilonwy's side. He touched her shoulder. The girl stirred, turned her face away, and murmured in her sleep.

"Quickly!" Taran whispered. "Gwydion waits for us."

Eilonwy roused, passed a hand over her forehead, and opened her eyes. At the sight of Taran she gave a cry of surprise.

"Gurgi is here, too," Taran said. "Fflewddur, Prince Rhun—all of us. You are safe. Hurry!"

"That's very interesting," said Eilonwy sleepily. "But who are they? And for the matter of that," she added, "who are you?"

CHAPTER XVI

A Meeting of Strangers

I am Eilonwy Daughter of Angharad Daughter of Regat," continued Eilonwy, putting her hand to the silver crescent at her throat. "But who are you?" she repeated. "I haven't the least idea in the world what you're talking about."

"Wake up," Taran cried, shaking her. "You're dreaming."

"Why, yes, as a matter of fact I was," Eilonwy answered, with a vague and sleepy smile. "But how did you guess? I don't believe dreaming actually shows when you're doing it." She paused, frowning. "Or does it? Sometime I shall have to find out. The only way, I suppose, is to look at myself when I'm asleep. And how I might go about that, I can't imagine." Her voice faltered and trailed away; she seemed suddenly to forget Taran was even there and sank back to the couch. "Difficult—difficult," she murmured. "Like trying to turn yourself inside out. Or would it be outside in?"

"Eilonwy, look at me!" Taran tried to raise her, but Eilonwy, with a little cry of annoyance, drew away. "You must listen," Taran insisted.

"That's what I've been doing," she replied. "So far you've made no sense whatever. I was much more comfortable asleep. I'd rather dream than be shouted at. But what was I dreaming? A pleasant dream—with a pig in it—and someone who—no, it's gone now, faster than a butterfly. You've spoiled it."

Taran had forced the girl to sit upright once more. Now he stared at her with dread. Despite her travel-stained garments and disheveled hair, she appeared unharmed. But her eyes were strangely depthless. It was not sleep that filled her, and his hands trembled as he realized Eilonwy had been drugged or—his heart chilled at the thought of it—bewitched.

"Listen carefully," he pleaded. "There is no time . . ."

"I don't believe people should be allowed to come stamping into other people's dreams without asking first," Eilonwy said, with some vexation. "There's something impolite about it. Like walking into a spider web when the spider's still using it."

Taran ran to the casement. He could see nothing of the companions below, nor any sign of Kaw. The moon was down and the sky would soon lighten. Quickly he turned back to Eilonwy.

"Make haste, I beg you!" he cried. "Climb down with me. The rope is strong enough for both of us."

"A rope?" exclaimed Eilonwy. "Me? Go sliding down with you? I've only known you these few moments, but it seems to me you make the silliest suggestions. No, thank you." She stifled a yawn. "You might try sliding down the rope yourself," she added with a certain sharpness, "and let me go back to sleep. I hope I can remember where I left off. That's the worst of having your dream broken into. You can never find it again."

Taran, sick with alarm, knelt beside her. "What holds you?" he whispered. "Fight against it. Can you not remember me? Taran, Assistant Pig-Keeper . . ."

"How interesting," remarked Eilonwy. "Some-time you must tell me more about yourself. But not now."

"Think," Taran urged. "Remember Caer Dall-ben—Coll—Hen Wen . . ."

Through the casement the sea wind carried trails of mist like tangled vines. Taran spoke the names again and the names of the companions.

Eilonwy's glance was so distant that she herself seemed far from the chamber. "Caer Dallben," she murmured. "How curious—I think that might have been part of my dream, too. There was an orchard; the trees were in blossom. I was climbing up, as high as I could go . . ."

"Yes, so it was," Taran pressed eagerly. "I, too, remember the day. You said you'd climb to the very top of the apple tree. I warned you not to, but you did anyway."

"I wanted to learn the trees," Eilonwy went on. "You must learn them anew every year," she said, "for they are always different. And in the dream I'd gone to the last branch."

"It was no dream," Taran urged, "but the life you know; your own life, not a shadow that vanishes in the sun. Indeed, you went to the highest branch. It snapped, as I feared it would."

"How should anyone know someone else's dream?" said Eilonwy, as though speaking to herself. "Yes, it broke and I was falling. There was someone below who caught me. Could it have been an Assistant Pig-Keeper? I wonder what became of him?"

"He is here now," Taran said quietly. "He has long sought you and in ways even he himself did not know. Now that he has found you, can you not find your path back to him?"

Eilonwy rose to her feet. Her eyes flickered and for the first time a light shone in them. Taran held out his hands to her. She hesitated, then took a step forward.

But even as she moved to him, her glance turned shallow and the light died. "It is a dream, no more than that," she whispered, and turned away.

"Achren has done this to you!" Taran cried. "She will harm you no longer." He seized the girl's arm and drew her toward the casement.

At the sound of Achren's name, Eilonwy stiffened and tore herself from him. She spun to face him. "You dare touch a Princess of the House of Llyr?"

Her voice was sharp; her eyes had lost their warmth; and Taran saw the brief moment of recollection had fled. He knew that Eilonwy, at all costs, must be taken from this dread place. His terror and dismay grew with the thought that perhaps even now she was beyond hope. He struggled to catch her by the waist and put her over his shoulder.

Eilonwy struck him full in the face with such force that he staggered back. Yet it was not the blow that pained him but her scornful glance. On her lips now was a smile of mockery and malice. He was a stranger to her and he feared his heart would break.

Once more he tried to seize her. Eilonwy, with a cry of rage, twisted away and broke free.

"Achren!" she called. "Achren! Help me!"

She ran to the portal of the chamber and into the corridor. Taran snatched up the rush light and raced after the fleeing Princess. Her sandals clattered down the shadowed hallway, and he glimpsed an edge of her robe vanishing around a corner. She had not ceased to call Achren's name. In another moment the castle would be roused and the companions discovered. Taran cursed himself for a blunderer. He had no choice now but to overtake the bewitched girl before every hope of escape faded. Already he heard a shout from the wall and the clash of blades.

The rush light scorched his hand and he cast it aside. In the darkness he sped to the end of the corridor and flung himself down a flight of steps. The Great Hall of Caer Colur stretched before him, the crimson haze of daybreak filling its ruined casements. Eilonwy fled across the wide stretch of worn and crumbling flagstones and vanished again. A hand gripped his jacket and spun him around. A torch flared in his eyes.

"The Pig-Keeper!" hissed Magg.

The Chief Steward plucked a dagger from a fold of his garments and thrust at Taran, who flung up an arm to ward off the blow. The dagger glanced aside. Magg cursed and swept the torch like a sword. Taran fell back, seeking to draw his own weapon. The shouts of the awakened guards filled the Great Hall. In another instant he caught sight of Gwydion, the companions at his heels.

Magg spun around. Fflewddur had broken away from the press of warriors and was racing at top speed toward the Chief Steward. The bard's spiky yellow hair streamed behind him and his face shone with furious triumph.

"The spider is mine!" cried Fflewddur, his blade whistling about his head. Magg, at the sight of the frenzied bard, yelled in terror and tried to flee. The bard was upon him in a moment, striking right and left with the flat of his sword in such a wild on-slaught that most of his blows missed their mark. Magg, with the strength of desperation, sprang at the bard's throat and grappled with him.

Before Taran could come to Fflewddur's aid, a warrior with an axe beset him and, despite his stout defense, Taran found himself driven back toward a corner of the Hall. Amid the confusion of the fray, he saw Gwydion and Rhun struggling against other war-riors. The Prince of Mona laid about him furiously with his broken sword, and it was to one of Rhun's sharp blows that Taran's assailant fell.

Fflewddur and Magg were still locked in com-bat. As Taran raced to the side of the bard, the dark, shaggy form of Gurgi overtook him. With a yelp of rage, Gurgi leaped into the air and clung to Magg's shoulders. The Chief Steward still wore his silver chain of office; Gurgi snatched it and let himself swing free. Magg gasped and tumbled backward, choking and hissing while Gurgi dangled for an instant, then sprang clear of the falling Steward. In a flash the bard was upon the prostrate Magg. Heedless of the buffeting from Magg's flailing legs, Gurgi laid hold of him by the heels and hung on with all his strength, while Fflewddur, sitting on Magg's head, seemed indeed to be carrying out his threat of squashing the treacherous Chief Steward.

Gwydion, with Dyrnwyn unsheathed and blazing, had cut down two warriors who now sprawled motionless on the flagstones. Terrified at the sight of the flaming weapon, the remaining guards fled. With long strides Gwydion hastened to the companions.

"Eilonwy is bewitched!" Taran cried. "I have lost her."

Gwydion's eyes went to the end of the hall where scarlet draperies had been flung back from an alcove. Eilonwy stood there and beside her, Achren.

CHAPTER XVII

The Spells of Caer Colur

Taran's heart froze, and within him echoed the nightmare memory of another day when he had stood in terror before Achren. As if he were still the same frightened lad he had been, he trembled once again at the sight of the black-robed Queen. Her hair, unbound, fell in glittering silver tresses to her shoulders; the beauty of her features had not changed, though her face was deathly pale. At Spiral Castle, long ago, she had been decked in jewels; now, neither rings nor bracelets adorned her slender hands and white arms. But her eyes, hard as jewels themselves, drew Taran's gaze and held it.

Gwydion had sprung forward. With a cry Taran followed him, sword upraised. Eilonwy shrank back and clung to Achren.

"Put down your weapons," Achren commanded. "The girl's life is bound to mine. Would you take my life? Then she must share my death."

Seeing the black sword, Achren had stiffened, but made no move to flee. Instead, her lips curled in the shadow of a smile. Gwydion halted and looked searchingly at her. Slowly, his face dark with anger, he returned Dyrnwyn to its sheath.

"Obey her," he murmured to Taran. "I fear Achren speaks the truth. Even in death she may be deadly."

"You show wisdom, Lord Gwydion," Achren said softly. "You have not forgotten me, nor have I forgotten you. I see, too, the Assistant Pig-Keeper and the foolish bard who should have been food for carrion crows long before this. The others, perhaps, know me not as well as you do, but soon they shall."

"Unloose the Princess Eilonwy from your spell," said Gwydion. "Return her to us and you shall depart unhindered."

"Lord Gwydion is generous," Achren replied with a mocking smile. "You offer me safety when your own peril is greatest. You were rash even to set foot on Caer Colur. And now the more hopeless your plight, the bolder your words." Her glance lingered on him. "Pity that one such as you scorned to be my consort and rule with me when the chance was given.

"Unloose the girl?" Achren went on. "No, Lord Gwydion. She will serve me as I planned. My spells are not the only ones to bind her. You know her ancestry and the blood of enchantresses that flows in her veins. Caer Colur itself has long awaited its Princess. It calls to her, and so it ever shall, while one stone stands upon the other. This is her birthright; I do no more than help her claim it."

"You force her to claim it!" Taran burst out. "Eilonwy did not come willingly to Caer Colur. She does not stay willingly." His desperation drowned his caution and he could not keep himself from starting toward Eilonwy, who watched him curiously. Gwydion's hand on his shoulder drew him back.

"Is she indeed unwilling?" Achren raised her arm and gestured to the alcove where stood an ancient chest tall as Eilonwy herself. "I have shown her what this contains," Achren said. "All the implements of magic treasured up for her. Power such as she has never known lies within her grasp. Do you ask her to cast it away? Let her give you her own answer."

At Achren's words Eilonwy raised her head. Her lips parted, but she did not speak. Hesitating, she toyed with the silver chain around her neck.

"Hear me, Princess," Achren said quickly in a low voice. "They would deprive you of your heritage, of the enchantments that are yours by blood-right."

"I am a Princess of Llyr," Eilonwy said coldly. "I want what is mine. Who are these who would take it from me? I see the one who frightened me in my chamber. A keeper of pigs, so he claimed. The rest I do not know."

Gurgi's heart-rending wail filled the Great Hall. "Yes, yes, you know us! Oh, yes! Do not speak hurtful words to sad companions. You cannot forget! This is Gurgi! Humble, faithful Gurgi! He waits to serve wise Princess as he always did!"

Taran turned his face away. The grief of the wretched creature pained him even more than his own. Achren, watching Eilonwy carefully, nodded with satisfaction.

"And their fate?" Achren said to her. "What shall be the fate of those who seek to despoil the inheritance of a Princess?"

Eilonwy frowned. Her eyes strayed over the companions. As though perplexed and reluctant, she turned to Achren. "They—they shall be punished."

"She speaks with your voice," Taran shouted in anger. "With your words! In her heart she does not wish us ill."

"Think you so?" replied Achren, taking Eilonwy's arm and pointing to Magg, prostrate on the flagstones and firmly in the grasp of the bard. "Princess, one of your loyal servants is still captive of these intruders. Cause him to be released."

Fflewddur, sitting astride Magg's shoulders, took a tighter grip on the scruff of the Chief Steward's neck. Magg spat and cursed while the bard shook him furiously. "Your trained spider is my prisoner!" Fflewddur cried. "He and I have business together, long unsettled. Do you want him back unsquashed? Then let the Princess Eilonwy come with us."

"I have no need to bargain," Achren answered. She made a curt gesture to Eilonwy. The girl's face, Taran saw, had taken on a harsh and severe expression; she lifted her arm, hand outstretched and fingers pointing.

"Which shall it be?" mused Achren. "The ill-favored creature who dared call himself your servant?"

Gurgi raised his head, puzzled and fearful, while Achren whispered words in a strange language to Eilonwy. The girl's fingers moved slightly. Gurgi's eyes widened in surprise and disbelief. For an instant he stood unmoving and open-mouthed, staring at the Princess. Her hand, pointing straight at the baffled Gurgi, suddenly tensed. With a sharp cry of pain, Gurgi stiffened and clutched his head.

Achren's eyes glittered with pleasure. Again she whispered urgently to Eilonwy. Gurgi shrieked. He spun frantically, his arms flailing as though to ward off unseen tormentors. Screaming, he flung himself to the ground, doubled up, and rolled back and forth. Taran and Gwydion raced to his side; but the tortured creature, like a wounded animal, struck at them and thrashed blindly in agony.

Fflewddur leaped to his feet. "No more!" he shouted. "Harm Gurgi no longer! You shall have Magg. Take him!"

At Achren's command, Eilonwy dropped her hand to her side. Gurgi lay gasping on the stones. His body shook with sobbing. He raised his shaggy, disheveled head, and Taran saw his face streaming with tears that came not only from the suffering he had just undergone. Painfully, the exhausted creature drew himself up to crouch on hands and knees.

Gurgi crept forward a little way. His weeping eyes turned to Eilonwy. "Wise Princess," he murmured, "it is no wish of hers to fill poor tender head with harmful hurtings. Gurgi knows this. He forgives her."

Magg, meantime finding himself free of the bard's grasp, lost no time in scrambling to his feet and scuttling to the side of Achren. His encounter with Fflewddur had left the Chief Steward much the worse for wear. His handsome garments showed rips and rents, his lank hair fell damply over his forehead, his chain of office was bent and battered. Nevertheless, once near Achren, Magg folded his arms and haughtily threw back his head; rage and hatred filled his eyes, and Taran was certain that had Achren given him the power Magg's glance alone would have sufficed to send Fflewddur rolling in torments sharper than Gurgi's.

"You shall pay dearly for this, harper," Magg spat. "I rejoice that I did not have you thrashed and driven away when first I laid eyes on you; for now it allows me to hang you in your own harp strings, from the highest tower of Rhuddlum's castle. And so shall I do, once I am Lord of Dinas Rhydnant."

"Lord of Dinas Rhydnant!" Fflewddur exclaimed. "A steward's chain is too much honor for you."

"Tremble, harper!" sneered Magg. "Dinas Rhydnant is mine. It has been promised me. And all the realm. King Magg! Magg the Magnificent!"

"King Magg the Maggot!" the bard flung back at him. "Does Achren promise you a kingdom? A scullery would be more than you deserve!"

"Achren's promises are false," cried Taran. "Learn this to your grief, Magg!"

The black-robed Queen smiled. "Achren 176 knows how to reward those who serve her, as she knows how to punish those who defy her. Magg's kingdom shall stand among the mightiest in the land. And Caer Colur shall rise more glorious than ever. Its Great Hall shall be the seat of power over all Prydain. The Lord of Annuvin himself shall kneel in homage to me." Achren's voice fell nearly to a whisper; a cold fire burned over her pale features. Her eyes were no longer on the companions, but far beyond them. "Arawn of Annuvin shall cower and beg for mercy. But his throne shall be toppled. It was I, Achren, who showed him the secret ways to power. He betrayed me and now he shall suffer my vengeance. It was I who ruled Prydain before him and none dared question my dominion. Thus shall it be once more. Thus shall it be evermore."

"The lore tells of your ancient rule," Gwydion said sharply, "and how you sought to keep hearts and minds in thrall to you. You tormented those who would not worship you; and for those who bowed to you, life was little better than a slow death. I know, too, of the blood sacrifices you demanded and your joy at the cries of your victims. No, Achren, it shall not come again. Think you this girl shall lead you to it?"

"She will obey me," Achren replied, "as surely as if I held her beating heart in my hand."

Gwydion's eyes flashed. "Your words are vain, Achren. They cannot deceive me. Do you seek to rule through the Princess Eilonwy? The enchantments she commands still sleep. You have not the means to waken them."

Achren's face turned livid and she drew back as though she had been struck. "You speak beyond your knowledge."

"Oh, no, he doesn't!" burst out Rhun, who had been listening in amazement. The Prince of Mona triumphantly faced Achren. "The book! The golden light! We've got them and we shall never give them up!"

CHAPTER XVIII

The Golden Pelydryn

Prince Rhun! Be silent!" Taran's warning came too
late. Rhun himself realized his blunder and clapped
a hand to his mouth; his round face filled with dismay
and he glanced about him in confusion. Gwydion
stood silently, his weathered features tight and pale;
yet the glance he cast on the unhappy Prince of Mona
was not of reproach but of sorrow. Prince Rhun's
shoulders drooped; he bowed his head and turned
wretchedly away.

Before Rhun's outburst, while Gwydion had
been speaking, Taran had sensed a shadow of fear
over Achren. It had passed now and her lips parted
in a subtle smile.

"Do you think I wish to hide the truth from
you, Lord Gwydion?" she said. "I knew the book of
spells had vanished from Caer Colur and I have long
sought it. The Golden Pelydryn was cast away or lost
by the Princess herself. Indeed, to fulfil my plan only
these objects are lacking. Accept my thanks, Lord
Gwydion," Achren went on. "You spare me the labor
of a tedious search. Spare yourself much pain by

putting them in my hands. Now!" she commanded harshly. "Give them to me."

Gwydion's voice was firm and his words came slowly and carefully. "It is as the Prince of Mona says. We have found the book of spells and the light that reveals them. But it is also as he says; you shall never have them."

"Shall I not?" replied Achren. "It is as simple as reaching out."

"They are not in our possession," Gwydion answered, "but well-hidden and beyond your grasp."

"That, too, is easily righted," said Achren. "There are means that will cause tongues to be loosened and the deepest secret shouted aloud." She glanced at Prince Rhun. "The Prince of Mona speaks even without my urging. He shall speak again."

Rhun blinked and swallowed hard, but he faced Achren stoutly. "If you're thinking about torturing me," he said, "you're welcome to try it. It would be interesting to see how much you could find out, since I myself haven't the first idea where the Pelydryn is." He took a deep breath and shut his eyes tightly. "So there you are. Go ahead."

"Give the harper to me, Lady Achren," Magg said eagerly, while Fflewddur bristled and stared defiantly at him. "He shall sing better to my music than ever he sang with his harp."

"Hold your tongue, Chief Steward," Achren snapped. "They shall speak willingly enough before I have done with them."

Gwydion's hand went to the hilt of the black

sword. "Harm none of my companions," he cried. "Do so and I vow to strike you down whatever the cost."

"Thus do I vow!" Achren flung back. "Seek to defeat me and the girl shall die!" Her voice lowered. "And so we stand, Gwydion, life against life and death against death. Which shall you choose?"

"If they have taken my bauble," said Eilonwy, drawing closer to Achren, "they must return it. It is not fitting for it to remain in the hands of strangers."

Taran could not hold back a cry of sorrow at Eilonwy's words. Achren, who had been studying the face of each companion, turned quickly to him.

"This does not please you, Assistant Pig-Keeper," she murmured. "It pains you to be called stranger by her. It cuts more cruelly than a knife, does it not? Sharper even than the torments of the wretched creature at your feet. She will remain thus because I so command it. Yet I could give back her memory of you. Is a golden trinket too high a price? Or a book of spells that are meaningless to you?"

Achren drew closer to Taran, fixing him with her eyes. Her voice had dropped to a whisper; her words, seeming to reach him alone, twined around his heart. "What cares an Assistant Pig-Keeper whether I or another hold sway over Prydain? Lord Gwydion himself cannot gain for you what you hold dearest; indeed, he can bring about only her death. But I can give you her life. Yes, a gift only I can bestow.

"And more, much more," Achren whispered. "With me, the Princess Eilonwy shall be a queen. But who shall be her king? Would you have me set her free to wed a witless Prince? Yes, Magg has told me she is to be given to the son of Rhuddlum.

"What then shall be the lot of an Assistant Pig-Keeper? To win a Princess only to lose her to another? Are these not your thoughts, Taran of Caer Dallben? Think of this, too, that Achren gives favor for favor."

Achren's eyes pierced him like dagger points and Taran's head whirled. Half-sobbing he tried in vain to stop his ears against the whispered words and buried his face in his hands.

"Speak now," Achren's voice went on. "The Golden Pelydryn—its hiding place . . ."

"You shall have what you ask!"

For an instant Taran thought it was his own voice crying out beyond his will to silence. Then he gaped in disbelief.

The words had come from Gwydion.

The Prince of Don stood with his wolf-gray head flung back, his eyes blazing, and on his face a look of wrath such as Taran had never seen before. The warrior's voice rang harsh and cold through the Great Hall, terrible to hear, and Taran trembled at the sound of it. Achren started in a sudden movement.

"You shall have what you ask," Gwydion cried again. "The Golden Pelydryn and the book of spells are buried at the broken wall near the gate, where I myself set them."

Achren was silent a moment, then her eyes narrowed. "Do you lie to me, Gwydion?" she murmured through clenched teeth. "If it is not true, the Princess Eilonwy will not live beyond this instant."

"They are within your reach," Gwydion replied. "Shall you hold back from taking them?"

Achren made a curt gesture to Magg. "Fetch them," she ordered. The Chief Steward hastened from the Hall and Achren turned once more to Gwydion. "Beware, Prince of Don," she said in a hoarse whisper. "Touch not your sword. Make no move toward us."

Gwydion did not answer. Taran and the companions stood motionless and speechless.

Magg had returned to the Great Hall. His sallow face twitched with excitement as he triumphantly bore aloft the Golden Pelydryn. Breathless, he ran to Achren's side. "So it is!" he cried. "They are ours."

Achren snatched the objects from him. The golden sphere was dull as lead, its beauty gone. She held it avidly; her eyes glittered; and her smile showed the white tips of her sharp teeth. For a moment she stood as though reluctant to part with the treasures she had sought, then pressed them into Eilonwy's hands.

Magg was beside himself with impatience and eagerness. He gripped his silver chain with clawed fingers, while his cheeks trembled and greed lit his beady eyes. "My kingdom!" he cried, in a tight, high-pitched voice. "Mine! It shall soon be mine!"

Achren spun and faced him scornfully. "Silence! A kingdom, groveling fool? Be grateful if you are allowed to keep your life."

Magg's jaw dropped and his face turned the color of moldy cheese at the import of Achren's words.

Choking as much with terror as with rage, he cowered under Achren's threatening glance.

The book of spells lay open in Eilonwy's outstretched hand. She had taken the Golden Pelydryn and was looking at it curiously. In the depths of the golden sphere a tiny light like a whirling, blazing snowflake had begun to take shape. She frowned, and a strange expression came over her face. As Taran watched, horror-stricken, Eilonwy shuddered violently, her head flung from one side to the other as though in pain. For an instant her eyes opened wide and she appeared about to speak. Her voice was no more than a gasp. Yet in that fleeting moment it seemed to Taran she had regained some vague memory of herself. Was it his own name she had tried hopelessly to cry out? The girl swayed as if torn between mighty forces that stormed within her.

"Read out the spells!" Achren ordered.

Little by little the light of the Golden Pelydryn grew brighter. Throughout the Great Hall rose a faint, confused whispering, as though the wind had gained tongue, urging, cajoling, commanding. The very stones of Caer Colur seemed to have taken voice.

"Quickly! Quickly!" cried Achren.

Eilonwy, Taran realized in a surge of hope, was struggling against all that held her. The anguished girl was beyond all threats of Achren, beyond all help from the companions.

Then, suddenly, her lonely combat ended. Taran cried out in despair as Eilonwy raised the glowing sphere and in a quick motion brought it close to the empty pages.

The Golden Pelydryn flared brighter than he had ever seen it and Taran flung up his hand to shield his eyes. Light flooded the Hall. Gurgi threw himself to the ground and covered his head with his shaggy arms. The companions drew back fearfully.

Suddenly Eilonwy cast the book to the flag-stones. From the pages burst a crimson cloud that spread into a sheet of fire, leaping upward to the vaulted ceiling of the Great Hall. Even as the book of spells consumed itself in its own flames, the blaze did not dwindle but instead rose ever higher, roaring and crackling, no longer crimson but blindingly white. The shriveled pages swirled in a fiery whirlwind to dance within the shimmering heart of the flame, and as they did, the whispering voices of Caer Colur groaned in defeat. The scarlet curtains of the alcove blew outward, seized in the writhing column of fire. Now the book had vanished utterly, but still the flames mounted unappeased.

Achren was shrieking, shrieking in rage and frenzy, her face distorted with hopeless fury. Still clutching the Golden Pelydryn, Eilonwy crumpled and fell.

CHAPTER XIX

The Flood

Gwydion leaped forward. "Your power is ended, Achren!" he cried. The livid Queen staggered for an instant, then turned and fled screaming from the Great Hall. Taran raced to Eilonwy's side and, heedless of the flames, struggled to raise the girl's limp body. Gwydion sped to overtake Achren. The bard followed them, his sword drawn. Magg had vanished. Gurgi and Prince Rhun hastened to aid Taran. Within moments Fflewddur returned. His face was ashen.

"The spider tries to drown us!" he shouted. "Magg has opened the gates to the sea!"

As the bard called out, Taran heard a thunder of surf. Caer Colur trembled. Shouldering the unconscious Eilonwy, he stumbled through a ruined casement. Kaw circled frantically above the towers. Fflewddur was urging the companions toward the portals, where they might hope to gain the boat. Taran followed him only to see, in despair, the great iron-bound gates nearly ripped from their hinges by the pounding water. Shattered, they had swung inward, and the foaming tide rushed upon the island like a ravening beast.

Beyond the walls, at the crest of a driving wave, rode Achren's vessel, mast askew and sails flapping. The surviving warriors clung to the sides of the tossing craft and fought to climb aboard. At the bow stood Magg, his face contorted with hate, shaking his fist at the crumbling fortress. The wreckage of Gwydion's boat spun in the flood, and Taran knew all means of escape were shattered with it.

The outer walls crumbled under the first impact of the sea. Blocks of stone shuddered and split away. The towers of Caer Colur swayed, and the ground reeled under Taran's feet.

Gwydion's voice rang above the tumult. "Save yourselves! Caer Colur is destroyed! Jump clear of the walls or they will crush you!"

Taran saw that the Prince of Don had clambered to the highest rocks of the embankment to which Achren had fled. There, Gwydion strove to lead her from the collapsing stones, but she struck at him and clawed his face. Her shrieks and curses pierced the rumble of onrushing waves. Gwydion faltered and fell as the embankment gave way.

The last barrier of ruined wall toppled. A hissing sheet of water blotted out the sky. Taran clasped Eilonwy to him. The flood swept them away and bore them under. Salt foam choked him and the merciless buffeting of the tide nearly tore the unconscious girl from his arms. He struggled upward while the island split and sank in a whirlpool that clutched him. Gripping Eilonwy, Taran fought clear of the whirlpool only to fall prey to breakers tossing him like wild stallions.

He spun to the trough of the waves while the sea pounded strength and breath from him. Still, he was able to hope, for it seemed the white-crested breakers were bearing him and his frail burden closer to shore. Dizzied and half-blinded by the green-black waves, Taran caught a confused glimpse of beach and shallow surf. He struck out weakly with his free arm. But in this last effort his failing body betrayed him and he tumbled into darkness.

Taran awoke under a gray sky. The roaring in his ears was not the surf. Two enormous yellow eyes peered into his own. The roaring grew louder. Hot breath was on his face. As Taran's sight cleared, he saw sharp teeth and a pair of tufted ears. He realized in confusion that he was lying flat on his back and Llyan was standing over him with one huge, padded paw on his chest. He cried out in alarm and struggled to free himself.

"Hullo, hullo!" Prince Rhun was now bending over him, a wide grin on his round face. Beside him was Fflewddur. The bard, like Rhun, was soaked and bedraggled, and strands of dripping seaweed hung from his yellow hair.

"Steady, now," said Fflewddur. "Llyan means you no harm. She only wants to be friendly, though sometimes she has odd ways of showing it." He patted the cat's great head and scratched under her mighty jaws. "Come, Llyan," he coaxed, "there's a good girl. Don't stand on my friend; he's not up to it yet. Behave yourself and I'll play you a tune as soon as my harp strings dry."

Fflewddur turned once more to Taran. "We have to thank Llyan for a great deal. Everything, in fact. She fished us all out of the surf after the sea had washed us up. If she hadn't, I'm afraid we should still be there."

"It was really surprising," put in Prince Rhun. "I thought for certain I'd been drowned, and the curious thing was I couldn't notice any difference!"

"I did have a start when I came to my senses with Llyan sitting beside me," said Fflewddur. "She had my harp between her paws, as though she couldn't wait for me to wake up and begin again. The creature is mad about my music! That's why she tracked us all the way here. And, Great Belin, I'm glad she did! But I think she's finally understood there's a time and place for everything. She's really been quite gentle," he added, as Llyan began to rub her head against him with such vigor the bard could hardly keep his balance.

"Where are the others?" Taran interrupted anxiously.

"Kaw, I fear, is nowhere to be found. Gurgi's gone looking for driftwood to build a fire," replied the bard. "Poor creature, he's still terrified of Llyan. But he'll get used to her. I've grown quite fond of her myself. It's not often one finds such a good listener, and I think I shall keep her. Or," he added, while Llyan nuzzled her whiskers on his neck and gripped the bard with her powerful paws, "perhaps I should put it the other way around."

"What of Eilonwy, of Gwydion?" Taran pressed.

The bard's glance fell. "Yes, well," he murmured, "they're here. Gwydion has done all he can."

With mounting anxiety Taran rose unsteadily to his feet. In the lee of a tumble of rock Gwydion knelt beside two forms. Taran stumbled across the beach. Gwydion looked up at him, his face filled with concern.

"Eilonwy lives," he said, answering the question in Taran's eyes. "More than that I cannot say. This much I know: Achren no longer holds her."

"Achren—Achren is dead, then?" Taran asked. He stared at the black-shrouded figure.

"Achren, too, lives," answered Gwydion, "though long she hung between life and death. But her power is broken now. This is the answer to the riddle, yet I did not know it until I stood before her in the Great Hall. At first, I was not certain. When I understood that she would truly let herself go down to death before giving up Eilonwy, I knew she had lost command of all but the least of her own enchantments. I read it in her eyes and in her voice. Her day had begun to wane from the moment she had broken with the Lord of Annuvin.

"The spells of Caer Colur were her last hope. Now they are gone and Caer Colur lies at the bottom of the sea," Gwydion added. "We need fear Achren no longer."

"I fear her still," Taran said, "and I shall not forget Caer Colur. Achren spoke the truth to me," he went on quietly. "I had not the strength to listen to her any longer. I feared I would tell the hiding place of the Pelydryn—and hoped you would slay me before I did. Yet," Taran added, puzzled, "it was you yourself who spoke."

"It was a risk that had to be taken," Gwydion replied. "I had suspected something of the nature of the bauble; as it alone could reveal the spells, so it alone could destroy them. Only then could Eilonwy be free. At what cost to herself, I could not be sure. Alas, she has suffered deeply and grievously, perhaps too much."

"Dare we waken her?" Taran whispered.

"Touch her not," said Gwydion. "She must waken of herself. We can only wait and hope."

Taran bowed his head. "I would have given my life to keep her from harm, and I would give it now to spare her this." He smiled bitterly. "Achren asked what shall be the lot of an Assistant Pig-Keeper? It is a question I have often asked myself. I see now the life of an Assistant Pig-Keeper is of little use or import. Even to offer it for someone else is of no avail."

"Prince Rhun would gainsay you," Gwydion answered. "Without you, he would have wandered lost and in mortal danger."

"I swore an oath to King Rhuddlum," Taran replied. "I did not break it."

"And had you not sworn an oath," Gwydion asked, "would you not have done the same?"

Taran was silent for a while, then he nodded. "Yes, I believe I would. It was more than my oath that bound me. He needed my help, as I needed his." He turned to Gwydion. "I remember, too, when a Prince of Don aided a foolish Assistant Pig-Keeper. Is it not fitting now for the Pig-Keeper to aid a Prince?"

"Whether it be Prince or Pig-Keeper," said Gwydion, "such is the way of a man. The destinies of men are woven one with the other, and you can turn aside from them no more than you can turn aside from your own."

"And you, Lord Gwydion," came Achren's voice, "you have put a cruel destiny upon me."

The black-cloaked figure had risen. Achren clung to the rocks to bear herself up. Her face, half-hooded, was drawn and haggard and her lips were pale. "Death would have been a kindness. Why did you deny it to me?"

Taran shrank back as the once-haughty Queen raised her head. For an instant he saw her eyes flame again with pride and fury.

"You have destroyed me, Gwydion," she cried. "Do you hope to see me grovel at your feet? Are my powers indeed stripped away?" Achren laughed harshly. "One last remains to me."

It was then Taran saw she held a weathered branch of driftwood. She lifted it high and Taran gasped as in her hands it blurred and shimmered. Suddenly in its place was a dagger.

With a shout of triumph Achren plunged it toward her own breast. Gwydion sprang to her and seized her wrists. Achren fought against him as he tore the blade from her grasp. Once more the dagger became driftwood, which Gwydion snapped in two and cast away. Achren fell sobbing to the sand.

"Your enchantments have ever been the enchantments of death," said Gwydion. He knelt and gently placed a hand on her shoulder. "Seek life, Achren."

"No life remains to me but that of an outcast," cried Achren, turning from him. "Leave me to myself."

Gwydion nodded. "Find your own path, Achren," he said softly. "Should it lead you to Caer Dallben, know this: Dallben will not turn you away."

The sky had grown heavy with clouds; and, though it was little past midday, the high crags rising at the shore seemed purple with dusk. Gurgi had built a fire of driftwood and the companions sat silently near the sleeping Eilonwy. Farther down the beach, Achren, muffled in her cloak, crouched alone and unmoving.

For all that morning, Taran had not left Eilonwy's side. Fearful she might never wake and fearful, too, that she might waken as a stranger to him still, he did not rest from his weary vigil. Gwydion himself could not foretell how long-lasting was the harm that had been done her.

"Do not lose heart," Gwydion said. "It is good that she sleeps and more healing to her spirit than any potion I could give her."

Eilonwy stirred restlessly. Taran started up.

Gwydion put a hand on his arm and gently drew him back. Eilonwy's eyelids fluttered. Gwydion, his face grave, watched closely as her eyes opened and she slowly raised her head.

CHAPTER XX

The Pledge

The Princess sat up and looked curiously at the companions.

"Eilonwy," Taran whispered, "do you know us?"

"Taran of Caer Dallben," said Eilonwy, "only an Assistant Pig-Keeper could ask a question like that. Of course I know you. What I *don't* know is what I'm doing soaking wet and covered with sand on this beach."

Gwydion smiled. "The Princess Eilonwy has come back to us."

Gurgi shouted with joy and in that instant Taran, Fflewddur, and Prince Rhun began talking all at once. Eilonwy clapped her hands over her ears.

"Stop, stop!" she cried. "You're making my head swim. Listening to you is more confusing than trying to count your fingers and toes at the same time!"

The companions forced themselves to be silent while Gwydion quickly told her all that had happened. When he had finished, Eilonwy shook her head.

"I can see you had a much more interesting time than I had," she said, scratching Llyan's chin as the immense cat purred with pleasure. "Especially since I don't recall much of it.

"Too bad that Magg escaped," Eilonwy went on. "I wish he were here now. I should have a few things to take up with him. That morning when I was on my way to breakfast, he came looming out of one of the corridors. He told me something very serious had happened and I was to come with him immediately."

"If only we could have warned you," Taran began.

"Warned me?" Eilonwy replied. "Of Magg? I knew straight off, from the very look of him, he was up to something."

Taran stared at her. "And yet you went with him?"

"Naturally," said Eilonwy. "How else was I going to find out? You were so busy sitting in front of my chamber and threatening to have a guard put round me. I knew there was no use trying to get any sense out of you."

"Do not judge him harshly," said Gwydion, smiling. "He thought only to protect you. He was under my orders to do so."

"Yes, I realize that," said Eilonwy, "and I soon began to wish all of you had been with me. By then it was too late. We'd no sooner got clear of the castle than Magg tied me up. And gagged me! That was the worst of it! I couldn't speak a word!

"But it spoiled his own scheme," she went on. "He had indeed waited in the hills until the searching party was far ahead of us. Then he dragged me into the boat. His shins will be black and blue for a while to come, I assure you. But I dropped my bauble. Since I was gagged, I couldn't make him understand I wanted it back.

"But it served him right. Achren was furious when she saw I didn't have it. She blamed Magg, and I'm surprised she didn't have his head off then and there. To me, she was very sweet and thoughtful, so I knew right away something disagreeable was to come.

"After that," Eilonwy continued, "Achren cast a spell over me and I remember very little. Until the bauble was in my hands once more. Then—then it was very strange. In the light of it, I could see all of you. Not with my eyes, really, but in my heart. I knew you wanted me to destroy the spells. And I wanted to, as much as you did.

"Yet, it was as though there were two of me. One did and one didn't want to give up the spells. I knew it was my only chance to become an enchantress, and if I gave up my powers then that would be the end of it. I suppose," she said softly to Taran, "I felt a little the way you did long ago in the Marshes of Morva, when you had to decide to give up Adaon's magic brooch.

"The rest of it wasn't pleasant." Eilonwy's voice faltered. "I'd—I'd rather not talk about that."

She was silent a moment. "Now I shall never be an enchantress. There's nothing left for me now except being a girl."

"That is more than enough cause for pride," Gwydion said gently. "For all you chose to sacrifice, you have kept Achren from ruling Prydain. We owe more than our lives to you."

"I'm glad the book of spells burned up," Eilonwy said, "but I'm sorry I lost my bauble. By this time it's surely floated far out to sea." She sighed. "There's nothing to be done about that. But I shall miss it."

As she spoke, Taran glimpsed a flickering movement against the dark gray sky. He leaped to his feet. It was Kaw, swooping landward at top speed.

"The last of our strays!" cried Fflewddur.

Llyan's ears pricked up, her long whiskers twitched, but she made no attempt to lunge for the crow. Instead, she rose to her haunches and purred fondly at the sight of her former opponent.

His feathers bedraggled and pointing every which way, Kaw fluttered above Eilonwy. Despite his disreputable appearance, he squawked and snapped his beak with enormous self-satisfaction. "Bauble!" Kaw croaked. "Bauble!"

From his claws the Golden Pelydryn dropped into Eilonwy's outstretched hands.

Gwydion at first had decided the companions should rest until morning, but Prince Rhun was eager to return to Dinas Rhydnant.

"There's a great deal to be done," he said. "I'm afraid we've let Magg look after things we should have seen to ourselves. There's more to being a Prince than I thought. I've learned that from an Assistant Pig-Keeper," he added, clasping Taran's hand, "and from all of you. And there's still most of Mona to be seen. If I'm ever to be King, I'm sure I should see it all. Though, I hope, in a rather different way. So if you don't mind, I should like to set out now."

Gurgi had no wish to linger anywhere near Caer Colur, and Fflewddur could hardly wait to show Llyan her new home in his own realm. Eilonwy insisted she was quite able to travel, and at last Gwydion agreed they would start without delay. He agreed, too, that they would pass by the cavern to see how Glew fared, for Taran still held to the promise he had made to help the wretched giant.

The ragged band made ready to leave the coast. Achren, finally consenting to voyage to Caer Dallben, walked slowly, withdrawn into her own thoughts, while Llyan frisked beside the bard, and Kaw sported overhead.

Eilonwy had gone for a moment to the edge of the surf. Taran, following her, stood as she watched the dancing waves.

"I thought I should have a last look at Caer Colur," Eilonwy said, "just to remember where it is. Or rather, where it isn't. I'm sorry, in a way, that it's gone. Outside of Caer Dallben, it was the only home I had."

"Once you are safe at Dinas Rhydnant," Taran

said, "I shall stay no longer on Mona. I had hoped, after all you'd been through, that—that you'd come back with us. But Gwydion is sure that Dallben meant for you to stay here. I suppose he's right. I can hear Dallben now: Being rescued has nothing to do with being educated."

Eilonwy said nothing for a while. Then she turned to Taran. "One thing more I remembered at Caer Colur: Dallben's saying that there was a time when we must be more than what we are. Can it be true that being a young lady is more important than being an enchantress? Perhaps that's what he meant. I shall have to find out for myself.

"So if I must learn to be a young lady, whatever that may be that's any different from what I am," Eilonwy continued, "then I shall try to learn twice as fast as those silly geese at Dinas Rhydnant and be home twice as soon. For Caer Dallben is my only real home now.

"Why, what's this?" Eilonwy cried suddenly. "The sea has given us a present!"

She knelt and from the foaming surf drew a battered object and stripped away the trailing seaweed. Taran saw an ancient battle horn, bound in silver with a silver mouthpiece.

Eilonwy turned it over in her hands and looked carefully at it. She smiled sadly. "It's all that's left of Caer Colur. What use it might be, I don't know and never shall. But if you promise not to forget me until we meet again, I promise not to forget you. And this shall be my pledge."

"I promise gladly," Taran said. He hesitated. "But what pledge have I to give you? I have none, other than my word."

"The word of an Assistant Pig-Keeper?" said Eilonwy. "That shall do very well indeed. Here, take it. Giving gifts is much nicer than saying farewell."

"And yet," Taran answered, "we must say farewell. You know that King Rhuddlum and Queen Teleria mean to betroth you to Prince Rhun."

"Indeed!" exclaimed Eilonwy. "Well, I assure you they shall do no such thing. There's limits to having people make up your mind for you. Rhun has certainly improved; I think this journey was the best thing that ever happened to him and someday he might even make a respectable sort of King. But as for being betrothed . . ." She stopped suddenly and looked at Taran. "Did you seriously think for a moment I would ever . . . ? Taran of Caer Dallben," she cried angrily, her eyes flashing, "I'm not speaking to you!

"At least," Eilonwy added quickly, "not for a little while."

ABOUT THE AUTHOR

Lloyd Alexander was born and brought up in Philadelphia, where he still lives. As a boy, one of his favorite pastimes was browsing in bookstores (it still is!) and one purchase he well remembers was a children's version of the King Arthur stories. That started his interest in tales of heroes and led him to the Mabinogion, the classic collection of Welsh legends, where he met such characters as Prince Gwydion Son of Don. Many years later, when working on his children's book, TIME CAT, Mr. Alexander started to include a Welsh episode, but his research revealed such riches that he decided to save them for another time. With TIME CAT finished, he delved into all sorts of volumes from anthropology to the writings of an eighteenth-century Welsh clergyman, and slowly the imaginary country of Prydain and its inhabitants flowered from the diverse elements of his research to appear in THE BOOK OF THREE (an ALA Notable Book), THE BLACK CAULDRON (runner-up for the 1966 Newbery Award) and now in THE CASTLE OF LLYR.

Readers who have enjoyed Mr. Alexander's partiality to cats as fittingly expressed in such books as MY FIVE TIGERS, PARK AVENUE VET, and TIME CAT will find particular satisfaction in the first appearance of a feline in Prydain in this book. In fact, Mr. Alexander claims that Llyan was "inspired by the letters of two literary-minded cats, denizens of the household of a certain editor. They insisted that in a land like Prydain the prototype of cat-greatness *must* exist—and it turned out they were right."